D0898095

THE PORT OF PERIL

By OTIS ADELBERT KLINE

"*The Earth-man attacked with the brilliant display of swordsmanship which had made him famous throughout all Zorovia.*"

Frontispiece.

THE PORT OF PERIL

BY

OTIS ADELBERT KLINE

Illustrated by J. ALLEN ST. JOHN

THE GRANDON COMPANY
PROVIDENCE, RHODE ISLAND

1949

H A L L A D A Y   I N C.
EAST PROVIDENCE 14, R. I.

CONTENTS

Contents

ILLUSTRATIONS

THE PORT OF PERIL

CHAPTER I

The Theft Of Vernia

PERHAPS THE FURNITURE AND DECORations of the personal apartment of Robert Grandon would have appeared bizarre to earthly eyes. Its paneled walls were hung with strange weapons and still stranger trophies of the battlefield and chase—prized treasures of a soldier and a hunter. Skins of marmelots, fiercest cats of the Zorovian fern forests, and tremendous bear-like monsters known as ramphs, magnificent specimens all, were flung on the floor. Cloud-filtered sunlight entered through two immense windows that reached from floor to ceiling, opening on a private balcony which overlooked the palace gardens.

A marmelot, carved from red wood and supporting a round top of polished crystal formed a table in the center of the room. Around it, in chairs carved in the representation of kneeling giants holding scarlet cushions which formed both seats and backs, were four men.

"The power of the Huitsen must be broken, and broken forever," cried Aardven, brawny, bull-necked ruler of Adonijar. And he banged his huge fist on the table for emphasis, causing the kova cups to dance and rattle.

Robert Grandon, former Chicago clubman who had fought his way to the throne of Reabon, mightiest empire of Venus, grimly nodded his assent, as did his two other guests, Ad, ruler of Tyrhana, and Zinlo, ruler of Olba. For the sake of privacy and comfort, he had dispensed with the rigid formality of the throne room, and received them in his own drawing room.

Ad of Tyrhana stroked his square-cut, jet black beard meditatively. Then he turned to Grandon. "I fear we have disturbed you at a most inopportune time. A man about to start on a honeymoon should not be annoyed with affairs of state. It was only after we learned of the latest outrage perpetrated by the yellow pirates, that Aardvan and I, who were awaiting Zinlo's return to Olba, decided to hurry here in one of his swift airships.

"When he heard that one of my ships of war, crippled by a storm and half sinking, was set upon by these yellow fiends, part of its crew massacred and the rest carried off prisoners, and my daughter Narine taken to I know not what fate, we felt that something must be done, and done quickly."

"And I heartily agree with you," said Grandon. "The imperial navy of Reabon is at your disposal. Do you have any plan of action to suggest?"

"I felt sure you would come in with us," said Ad, "especially after my talk with Zinlo this morning. As I have intimated previously, we must make our plans in secret, and carry them out as unobtrusively as possible. The Huitsenni have spies everywhere. They have the treasure to hire the vile traitors among our people who will sell their honor for personal gains, but because of their peculiar physical characteristics they can do no eavesdropping among us themselves."

"We should have two main objectives: to sink or capture every pirate ship that sails the seas of Zorovia, and to find and take the secret port of Huitsen. It is a port of missing ships and treasure, of slaves who were once citizens of our own and other lands, a port of peril to every man, woman, and child on this planet."

"Have you any idea where to look for this hidden port?" asked Grandon.

"We have no definite knowledge of its location, but the belief that it lies to the south has arisen from the fact that pirate fleets, leaving a scene of pillage, have almost invariably been observed to sail southward."

"I believe my flyers can locate it," said Zinlo, toying with his kova cup.

"It's a big world," boomed the gruff Aardvan, "and it will take a deal of flying, sailing, and marching to explore it all."

"Perhaps Mernerum will help us," suggested Ad.

"I take it," replied Grandon, "that you are unaware of the strained, or rather severed relations, between Mernerum and Reabon. This morning I ordered diplomatic relations severed with Zanaloth of Mernerum, because of his affront to my wife when she passed through his dominions some time ago."

"We can do well enough without that dissolute, old rake," said Zinlo. "But we're keeping you from that honeymoon trip, Grandon. I understand that your expedition was ready to march when Ad and Aardvan arrived."

"We'll give it up," Grandon assured them. "I'm sure Vernia won't mind for such a worthy cause."

"See here," Ad protested. "We don't want any such sacrifice. Allow us to take a few of your ships for the present, and perhaps some warriors and munitions in case a landing party is required. Go on your honeymoon. Later, when we've dis-

covered the port of peril, we'll notify you, and let you in at
the kill."

"But your daughter has been stolen. Every man on this
planet, worthy of the name, should be willing to assist in the
search."

Ad sighed deeply, musingly. "Alas," he replied, "I fear
all search for her will be vain. She has been gone for so
long now that I can only hope to avenge her. But, of course,
I, her father, shall continue to search." He arose, and continued: "My friends and allies, we have imposed long enough on
this patient, young bridegroom. I'm sure you will all agree
with me when I say that we don't want his help until after
the honeymoon. Let him lend us a few ships and men now,
and we'll call on him later."

"Those are precisely my sentiments," roared the deep-voiced
Aardvan, also rising.

"And mine," echoed Zinlo. "And so, Grandon, we'll go
down and join the group outside that's waiting to see you off.
By the way, where are you bound?"

"It was a toss-up whether to go to the wild mountain fast-
ness of Uxpo, or enjoy the bathing, fishing, and boating of the
Azpok coast. But the seashore won, and we chose a camping-
place on a wild and unfrequented part of the coast."

"Splendid! We'll see you outside."

A half-hour later, speeded by an immense multitude that had
lined the streets of Reabon to see them off, Grandon and his
young bride, Vernia, Princess of Reabon, stepped into the
waiting, one-wheeled motor vehicle, and with their guard of
Fighting Traveks, left for the coast.

In the imperial tent of scarlet silk, decked with cloth-of-gold
insignia and edged with golden fringe, Grandon opened his
eyes as the first faint dawnlight appeared, for he had planned
an early morning fishing-trip. He arose and dressed silently,
so as not to disturb the slumber of his bride, but she heard

the slight clank of his sword as he was about to step through the doorway, and wakened.

"Bob."

He turned as she softly pronounced the name by which he had been known to his friends on Earth, the name he had taught her to call him and which he loved to hear her say with her quaint, Reabonian accent.

With three steps he was at her bedside. She smiled up at him, the pink and white oval of her face framed in the wealth of golden ringlets that all but concealed her silken pillow. Then she held up both arms.

"Would you leave without kissing me good-bye?" she asked reproachfully.

Contritely, he knelt beside the bed and took her in his arms.

"I did not wish to disturb your morning sleep my dear," he said, and added: "I was only going out for a little while to have a try at a killer-norgal. I'm told they bite best at daybreak."

She took his face between her palms, drew it down to hers, and their lips met.

"Never leave me," she said, "without first kissing me good-bye. Who knows how long any separation may be? Even though we may expect to be parted for but a few moments, the hand of Providence may intervene and separate us for a long time—perhaps for eternity."

He buried his face in the soft curve of her neck as she ran her fingers through his black curls. Nor did he dream, as he held her thus for a few moments, how soon the dire prophecy in her words was to be fulfilled.

"I'll be back in a jiffy," he said, as he stood erect a few moments later.

She watched him, love and pride in her eyes, as he strode through the door. Handsome, strong, and gentle, he was an emperor—every inch of him.

Throwing a shimmering wrap of scarlet material around her, she went to the door of her tent to watch him depart. Two guards saluted stiffly as she appeared. They were members of a company of Grandon's crack troops, the Fighting Traveks from Uxpo. Each was armed with a tork, a rapid fire weapon that shot needle-like glass projectiles, a scarbo, a cutting and thrusting weapon with a basket hilt and a blade curved like that of a scimitar, and a long-bladed spear.

Vernia watched him for a few moments as he stood beside his small fishing-boat in earnest conversation with Huba, mojak or captain of the company of Traveks who were guarding the camp. Six men stood on each side of the little craft, holding it's nose into the breakers. In the prow of the boat was Kantar the Gunner, carefully shielding his mattork—a weapon resembling a tork, but of considerably heavier caliber and longer range, and mounted on a tripod— from the spray that was breaking over the bow, by holding a waterproof silk cover over it.

The rest of the crew consisted of six oarsmen, a man who had charge of the sail, and another who held the tiller.

Having finished his conversation with Huba, Grandon leaped into the craft, and the twelve men who were standing in the water launched her. When they reached water up to their necks, they let go, and the rowers plied their oars vigorously. Presently the sail went up, and the little boat tacked into the breeze which was just lively enough to stir the fog that hung low over the surface of the Azpok.

The princess watched the boat until the mists had swallowed it up, then turned and re-entered her tent. But scarcely, it seemed, had she crept once more beneath her warm covers, and closed her eyes in sleep, before there sounded outside the crack of a mattork, the shouts of men, and the clank of weapons, followed by a fusillade of shots that told her the camp was being attacked by a considerable body of armed men.

Jumping out of bed, Vernia called to the guard outside.

"What is it?" she asked. "What has happened?"

"Pirates, Your Majesty!" replied the guard excitedly. "We are attacked by the raiders of the coast."

She dressed as swiftly as possible, buckling the jeweled belt which held her small tork and scarbo around her slender waist. Meanwhile, the sounds of fighting drew closer and closer to the scarlet tent.

As soon as she was dressed, Vernia drew her scarbo and stepped fearlessly from the tent. Descended from a thousand fighting Torrogos, or Emperors, of Reabon, she was fully as brave as her mighty husband, even though she lacked his strength and skill in swordsmanship. With flashing eyes she surveyed the scene before her. Tugging at their anchors, less than a quarter of a mile from land, were a score of vessels which she instantly recognized from pictures she had seen as the ships of the dreaded yellow pirates, the scourge of the Azpok Ocean. Their peculiar sails, branching out on either side of the mast like the wings of bats, instantly identified them. And coming rapidly shoreward were no less than fifty boats loaded with armed men, each mounting a mattork in the bow. But this was not all, for converging on the camp from both sides and the rear was an immense horde of yelling, shooting pirates. Already, more than a third of the Fighting Traveks had fallen, and the tork and mattork fire from all directions was rapidly decimating the ranks of those who remained.

A dozen of the boats were sent down by Huba's mattork gunners before the landing-party reached the shore. As their prows grounded, the remaining pirates leaped out and charged the camp, and it was the signal for a general advance from all directions.

The camp had been guarded by two hundred men, but by the time of the charge, a scant forty remained. They formed a hollow square around the Princess, and met the shock of the attack with a resistance worthy of the traditions of the

Fighting Traveks, though it was obvious from the beginning that there could be but one outcome.

In the hand-to-hand fighting that followed there was no report of tork or mattork—only the clash of blades, the war-cries of the fighters, the groans of the wounded, and the shrieks of the dying. Vernia and Huba fought bravely with the others, time and again leaping into the gaps left by fallen men until the line could be closed. But they were wag-ing a hopeless fight, and presently only the Princess and the mojak were left, fighting back to back. The latter, battling three adversaries at once, was suddenly cut down by a blow from one of the pirates, and Vernia was left alone. When a man leaped in from behind, pinioning her arms, her weapons were quickly taken from her.

The looting of the camp was already in progress as she was dragged, kicking and struggling, into one of the pirate boats. Everything in the camp was seized in the way of booty except the bodies of the fallen Traveks, and even these were stripped of their clothing, weapons, and accouterments. The pirates also took with them all of their own dead and wounded.

Rowed to the largest of the looters' vessels, Vernia was car-ried aboard and taken before an officer whose insignia pro-claimed him romojak, or commander, of the fleet. Like most of the members of his race, he was short, scarcely taller than the Princess herself, but with an exceptionally long body and arms. His round, yellow face was seamed and wrinkled, and his equally round eyes, wide open and staring, were without irises. The pupils were perpendicular slits that opened and closed like those of felines. His short nose resembled the tip of a pig's snout, and there were no teeth in the chinless mouth be-neath it, from the corners of which drooled saliva reddened by the juice of the kerra, the spores of a narcotic, fungoid growth chewed almost incessantly by the yellow pirates. Nor was there a sign of beard, eyebrows, or hair on the face or head, the skin of his body being covered with a greasy exuda-

"*Then a man leaped in from behind, pinioning her arms,
and her weapons were quickly taken from her.*"

Chapter I.

tion, evidently nature's protection for these totally hairless people. Judged by the standards of his hairless, toothless race, he was probably not unhandsome. But to Vernia, facing him as his prisoner, he was a monstrosity.

"I presume you are the Torroga of Reabon," he said in patoa, with the peculiar pronunciation that a lack of teeth induces.

"You have already presumed too much," replied Vernia, spiritedly. "For this day's work, I can promise you the annihilation of the Yellow Pirates."

The gums of the romojak showed in a toothless grin. He expectorated a red stream of kerra juice, then turned to a short, bow-legged, pot-bellied mojak who stood beside him.

"Do you hear that, San Thoy?" he mouthed sneeringly. "I, Thid Yet, Romojak of the navies of Huitsen, have presumed too much!"

The mojak duplicated his kerra-stained grin.

"The Huitsenni never presume too much," he replied.

"Well said, San Thoy," approved the romojak. Then he addressed Vernia once more. "Your Majesty, the Huitsenni presume often, but never too much. Have they ever been beaten in battle? Has one of them ever been led to your court, a prisoner? Have their cities ever been found by pursuing battle fleets? Your Majesty is aware that history can answer but one word to these questions, and that word is: 'No'."

"There is only one reason why it must be so answered," replied Vernia. "Cowardice. You never attack unless your overwhelming numbers assure you of victory. For this reason you never lose battles or prisoners. Your cities have not been found because you are adepts at flight from an enemy. In this there is nothing of which to be proud."

"Your Majesty calls it 'cowardice'," said Thid Yet, "but we of the Huitsenni have a better word. We call it 'cleverness'. However, I am not here to bandy words with you, nor dis-

pute terms. You are my prisoner, captured not for myself,
but for another. If you are reasonably docile and do not attempt to escape, you will be treated with gentleness and courtesy. If not—whatever misfortune befalls will be upon your own
head." He turned to the greasy, pot-bellied mojak beside him.
"Take her to her cabin, San Thoy."

C H A P T E R II

GRANDON PURSUES

FAR OUT INTO THE MORNING MISTS that shrouded the surface of the blue-gray Azpok, Grandon sailed in search of the largest and most ferocious of all Zorovian game fish—the killer-norgal. Fishing for the norgal was royal sport indeed, and fraught with great danger to the fisherman. Hunting a full-grown man-eating tiger with a lariat could be no more dangerous, and as often as not, the man who lacked skill fell a prey to the fish.

Grandon had never seen a killer-norgal, and so when he felt a sharp tug at his trolling-line, and a magnificent specimen broke water, leaping high in the air and shaking its head to dislodge the hook, he had one of the greatest thrills that had ever come to him, intrepid adventurer though he was. Its body, covered with glistening blue scales and bristling with sharp spines, was about twenty-five feet in length. Its enormous jaws, when distended, revealed row upon row of sharp, back-curved teeth in a maw large enough to take in a dozen men at a single snap.

Kantar the Gunner jerked the oily cover from his mattork, but before he could bring it to bear on the huge fish, it dived out of sight.

Grandon kept a taut line on his quarry while the crew skillfully maneuvered the little craft to follow its eccentric and exceedingly swift motions as it dragged the boat farther and farther out to sea. After more than an hour of this, the struggles of the monster became slower, indicating that it was beginning to tire. During this time, it did not once expose itself to the deadly aim of the watchful Kantar.

Suddenly, without warning, the line slackened, and although Grandon reeled in with all his might, he was unable to pull it taut. He thought at first that the fish had become unhooked, but the flash of a dorsal fin, for a moment visible above the waves and coming swiftly towards the boat, showed him the true situation. Kantar's mattork spoke, and the fin disappeared, but it was not evident whether he had registered a hit.

One of the older sailors, an experienced norgal fisherman, said:

"Beware, Majesty. The killer is about to strike."

Dropping his tackle, Grandon seized an eighteen foot lance which lay along the gunwale beside him, and poised it expectantly. He had not long to wait, for the enormous jaws suddenly emerged from the water not ten feet from him. He plunged the keen point down the cavernous maw, and Kantar's mattork spoke again and again, while the mighty jaws ground the thick shaft of tough serali wood into splinters. Hurling the useless butt from him, Grandon whipped out his sword, but he sheathed it again as the great spiny body turned over and floated belly up after a few convulsive flops. The blood which poured out through one of the gills showed that the lance point had found the heart, and several round holes through the head attested the marksmanship of Kantar.

The sailors were making the prize fast, chattering and laughing all the while, when the keen-eared Kantar suddenly cried: "Listen, I hear shooting!"

Every voice was instantly hushed, and there came, distinctly now, the sounds of a terrific bombardment from the north.

"The camp is attacked," cried an old sailor.

"To the oars," ordered Grandon, "and crowd all the sail on at once. Cut that fish loose. We must get there as soon as possible."

The huge, spiny carcass was cast adrift, and sails and oars were speedily put into use. Yet, it seemed to Grandon that the swift little boat, which fairly leaped over the waves under this double propulsion moved with snail-like slowness.

Before they had gotten half-way back to camp, the sounds of firing ceased, and Grandon, goaded by horrible fears for Vernia's safety, fumed and fretted at the inability to make better speed or see through the mists that made about two hundred yards the limit of visibility.

But when the prow of the little boat grounded on the beach, and leaping out, Grandon discovered the bloody shambles that had been his camp, strewn with the naked bodies of his Traveks, his grief and anger knew no bounds.

"All dead," he said to Kantar, who stood respectfully beside him. "My noble Traveks slaughtered, and Vernia stolen. Who can have done this horrid deed? And what motive? Reabon is at peace with all nations. The camp was not rich in loot."

"There is Zanaloth of Mernerum," replied Kantar. "You have severed diplomatic relations with him. Perhaps this is his answer."

"If Zanaloth has done this," said Grandon, "he shall have war, and that speedily—such a war as this planet has never seen. I will wipe Mernerum off the face of the globe, nor will Zanaloth live long to gloat over his evil deeds. But it cannot be Zanaloth. The fact that he once affronted the Princess of Reabon when she passed through his country made it imperative that I sever diplomatic relations until full apology had been made. I might have declared war, but did not. Zanaloth should be thankful for this, as the armies of Reabon could crush a dozen Mernerums."

Walking among his dead Traveks and sorrowfully murmuring the names of those he recognized, Grandon presently found his mojak.

"My faithful friend," he said, sadly. "Huba, comrade of many a battle and bivouac." He knelt and laid his hand on the blood-smeared brow of the young officer. "Why, his head is warm!" he exclaimed. "Perhaps a spark of life remains! Fetch water and a flask of kova, quickly, Kantar."

The gunner sped away to the boat from which he brought back a flask of the aromatic and stimulating kova from the provision basket and a bailing-scoop of sea-water.

There was a huge gash in the fallen mojak's scalp, and the entire upper part of his face was covered with blood. With hands as gentle as those of a woman, Grandon bathed away the blood. Then, as the eyelids of his friend flickered, he raised the head and held the flask of kova to the mouth, forcing a a small quantity of the liquid between the clenched teeth.

Huba swallowed convulsively, opened his eyes, and looked at Grandon with dull wonder in his gaze.

"You, Majesty!" he said weakly. "I thought I had been taken to the bosom of Thorth."

"You came near it," replied Grandon, "but the scarbo cut was a glancing one. Where is my wife?"

"The cursed Huitsenni attacked the camp," answered Huba. "My valiant Traveks fought well, but were cut down to the last man. Her Majesty fought with us. When all had been killed around us, she and I fought the greasy yellow horde, back to back. Then I was cut down, and knew no more. What a brave little thing she is!" He sank back, exhausted.

"Then those yellow fiends have her," said Grandon. Their spies have worked swiftly it seems, and they were swift at reprisal. Where have they taken her? How can I follow?"

"I do not know," replied Huba, "nor do I believe anyone does, other than the pirates themselves. They raid the coasts or attack merchant or fishing ships, then disappear. As they always attack with immensely superior forces, they are never defeated. They always carry away their own dead and wounded, and take care that none of their victims are left alive to tell of their dastardly work. But a few times, men who have been left for dead have revived, even as I was revived, and thus some description of them and their deeds has, from time to time, reached civilization. Fleets of the great nations have scoured the seas, looking for their ships and their strongholds, but have found neither. Like the winds of heaven, no one knows whence they come or where they go."

"I'll find Vernia if I have to search every inch of this planet," said Grandon.

"One thing only I recall, which may be of assistance, Majesty," said Huba. "Unfortunately I was unable to see the pirates leave, but every intended victim who has ever escaped them has reported that they sail southward."

Grandon turned to the mojo of the boat crew.

"Remove all but two pairs of oars," he said, "and prepare to push off. I will sail southward. One man, only, will I take with me. Who would be the man?"

From the wounded Huba to the last of the seamen, all volunteered. After some deliberation, Grandon selected Kantar the Gunner as his companion.

"You will be needed in Reabon," he told Huba. "Go at once to the capital. Tell Vordeen to mobilize the army and double the coast guard and the guard on the Mernerum border. Tell him, also, to divide our war fleet into such sized squadrons as he deems advisable, and assign patrol zones to each squadron so that no part of the Azpok Ocean nor any of its shore line will be left unsearched. Have these patrol fleets search every ship encountered, except those of Tyrhana, Adonijar and Olba. Farewell."

The seamen echoed Huba's cry of: "Farewell, Majesty," as Grandon leaped into the boat and seized the tiller. Kantar, already at the oars, struck out savagely as soon as the men who shoved them off had got beyond their depth, and a little later, the two raised the sail and tacked into the breeze, which had grown considerably stronger. The fog, too, was rising so that visibility became almost normal.

For most of the morning they zig-zagged southward, but presently the wind veered around, eliminating the necessity for tacking, and greatly accelerating their progress.

At noon each took a turn at the tiller, while the other ate his frugal lunch of dried mushrooms and smoked frella meat washed down with drafts of kova.

Kantar had just finished his lunch, and was closing the watertight container when with an exclamation of surprise, he suddenly leaned over the gunwale and scooped something from the surface of the water with his hand. It was an empty half of a spore pod, red inside and black outside.

"What have you there?" asked Grandon.

"A kerra pod," replied the gunner.

"And what, pray, is that?"

"The kerra, Majesty," replied the gunner, "is chewed almost universally by the toothless yellow pirates. Where there are kerra spore pods, one may be sure the Huitsenni have been. It is said that they are never willingly without a supply of this habit-forming narcotic, which they constantly mumble except when eating or sleeping. I think from the finding of this kerra pod, that we are on the right trail—that the Huitsenni have passed this way not so long ago."

"And do you think there is a possibility of our overtaking them today?"

"I believe, Sire, that there is. This little boat is one of the fleetest on the Azpok—and much swifter than the large ships of war used by the pirates in their raids. They had not long been away from camp when we arrived, so I look for their appearance on the horizon some time this afternoon if they consistently follow their southward course."

That afternoon, Grandon constantly strained his eyes toward the south, but saw only such marine monsters of the Azpok as rose to the top from time to time, or flew above the surface. There was a great variety of web-winged reptiles of diverse shapes and colors, some as small as sea-gulls, and other kinds and species up to the enormous ormf, whose wing-spread was fully fifty feet from tip to tip, and whose great, saw-toothed beak with a pelican-like pouch beneath it was large enough to take in a full-grown man at a single snap. There was also a great profusion of large, white birds with hooked bills and red-tipped wings which, like the flying reptiles, dipped to the surface of the water from time to time for their prey, or dived beneath it, emerging therefrom with squirming, wriggling fish or other marine inhabitants in their beaks.

One huge ormf circled above the little craft for several hours, and Kantar prepared to use his mattork in case of attack. But the monster evidently decided that the creatures in the boat were too dangerous for it to assail, and soared lazily away.

Although they did not sight the ships of the pirates that afternoon, Grandon was encouraged by seeing, from time to time, empty kerra pods on the water, which indicated that they were on the right trail.

"The ships of the accursed Huitsenni," said Kantar as darkness fell, "must be swifter than I thought, or we should have sighted them before this."

Scarcely had he spoken when a sparkle of dancing lights appeared just above the southern horizon.

"I see lights to the south," said Grandon. "What are they?"

"The ships of Huitsen," replied Kantar, excitedly. "Those are their mast lights. We will overtake them shortly, now."

"And can you tell which is the flagship?" asked Grandon. "It will probably be on the ship of the leader that Her Majesty is confined."

"I will be able to tell which is the flagship when we get closer," replied Kantar, "by her lights."

"Good. As soon as you can do so, steer for the flagship. Make no noise, and perhaps we can get aboard without being seen. If we can do that—"

His speech was suddenly interrupted by a terrific shock, as the little boat, traveling through the inky darkness in which naught was visible except the dancing mast lights of the pirates, suddenly rammed a huge, solid object, throwing both men into the bottom of the boat.

The impact was followed by a terrific roar, and the front end of the fishing boat was lifted out of the water as easily as if it had been a floating chip, while Grandon and Kantar unable to see what they had struck, clung to such solid objects as they could grasp and breathlessly awaited the next move of the unseen monster.

C H A P T E R   III

The Cunning Of San Thoy

As SAN THOY LED VERNIA TO THE
cabin which had been assigned to her, his great round eyes,
with their cat-like pupils, appraised her in a manner which
made her fearful.

"Beauteous white princess," he said, when they were out of
earshot of Thid Yet and the group of pirates surrounding him,
"you are surrounded by enemies, yet San Thoy would be your
friend."

Weighing his look and words for a moment, Vernia asked:

"Just what do you mean?"

The slit pupils of his eyes narrowed, and this did not escape the observation of the Princess as he replied:

"I mean what I say, Majesty, in all sincerity. For the great respect and admiration I bear his Majesty, your husband, I would befriend you."

"You know my husband?"

"Only through the echoes of his mighty exploits, which have penetrated even to Huitsen," he replied. "But one brave man admires another, and feels a certain kinship with him. For his sake as well as for your own, I would be of assistance to you."

"In what way?"

"If you will give me your full trust and co-operation, I can help you to escape. If not, you will shortly be sold into slavery to a human monster whose mistreatment of the women who fall into his lascivious clutches has made him notorious throughout the length and breadth of Zorovia."

"Who?"

"I am under orders not to divulge his name, but we of the Huitsenni were offered an enormous sum in treasure and slaves for your safe delivery to him. It was for this reason and no other that our Rogo decided to brave the anger of that mighty fighter, your husband, and send a fleet to capture you at the wild and lonely spot where the spies of this licentious potentate had ascertained that you were but indifferently guarded."

"It seems strange that this dissolute monarch, whose name I believe I can guess, did not send his own ruffians instead of employing the Huitsenni," said Vernia.

"He feared the power of Reabon," replied San Thoy. "Any evidence which his own men might have left as to their presence on Reabonian soil would have led to war and the inevitable dissolution of his empire. For who can stand against the mighty hosts of Reabon? But who could criticize his perfectly legal action were he to buy a beautiful white slave-girl from the Huitsenni? And even though she should maintain that she were the Torroga of Reabon, what weight has the word of a slave? A thousand beautiful slave-girls might make the same assertion for their own advantage and advancement, and he would be legally privileged to disbelieve them. The man who ordered your capture, Majesty, is as clever as he is lecherous."

Vernia, who was familiar with the international laws of Venus, knew full well that no man could be held responsible under those laws for purchasing a slave. She knew, also, that it would be difficult to establish the fact in an international court that he was cognizant of the identity of that slave, whose word would have no legal weight, and could be doubted by him with impunity.

"Just what," she asked, "is your price?"

"My price is but a trifle," he responded. "In fact, it is scarcely worth mentioning."

"Name it."

"I should prefer to rescue you first."

They were standing before the door to the cabin to which he had led her, and which he had not yet unlocked. Suddenly both saw Thid Yet, Romojak of the fleet rounding a curve in the deck and coming toward them.

Quickly unlocking the door, San Thoy said:

"The Romojak comes. Go into your cabin, and I will call later."

Vernia stepped into a tiny cabin which contained a sleeping shelf that projected from the wall like the nest of a cave swallow, a small table, and a stool, both fastened to the floor. A ewer and a small bowl for washing were set in a niche in the wall.

As the door closed and the lock clicked behind her, she heard the approaching Thid Yet say:

"By what devious route did you take the prisoner to her cabin, San Thoy, that she but entered it?"

"I stood and talked to her for a moment, to cheer her," replied San Thoy humbly.

"To cheer her? Ha! So this little beauty has aroused your libidinous fancy! But it was to be expected. Understand me,

once and for all, San Thoy. This is no common slave-girl.
Her ransom is the price of a mighty empire, and she must be
delivered unharmed. Let me but suspect you, and you shall
die—very slowly and very painfully—mojak though you be."

"You misapprehend, Excellency," protested San Thoy. "Because I have spent my hard earned treasure for a few slaves
in the past, I pray you misjudge not my intentions toward
this one. I was moved to pity for her, that was all."

"You pity? Pah! Into your cabin with you, and lay our
course that we may reach Huitsen as soon as possible. And
do not forget my warning."

A moment later, Vernia heard the door of the cabin which
was next to hers, slam with unnecessary violence, and after
laving her face and hands with scented water from the ewer,
she lay down on her sleeping-shelf to rest, and to overcome
the giddiness which the rocking of the ship was beginning to
induce. But bad as were the qualms of sea-sickness, they
were as nothing as compared to her mental anguish, for she
felt that only a miracle could save her. Although she had
never been deceived by San Thoy's protestations of friendship,
she had been half ready to believe that an offer of treasure
might win his help. But the words of the Romojak had thoroughly dissipated even that slim hope.

Late that afternoon, San Thoy himself brought her food and
a bowl of kova. Because of her sea-sickness she could not
eat the food, but she drank the hot, steaming kova. Shortly
thereafter, she began to feel unaccountably drowsy, and soon
fell into a deep sleep.

When she awakened, Vernia felt the craft beneath her lurch-
ing and pitching violently. She put out a hand for the light
switch, but there was none. Instead, her hand encountered the
wet gunwale of a small boat, in the bottom of which she was
lying. She sat up, and the salt spray sprinkled her face. Far
away, she saw a number of mast lights twinkling in the darkness. A short bulky figure loomed up before her.

"Who are you?" she asked in terror. "Where are you taking me?"

"Have no fear, Majesty," mouthed the figure. "It is San Thoy that has rescued you."

"You drugged me."

"For your own sake, Majesty. You might otherwise have made an outcry when I came to carry you off, thus arousing the ship and defeating your rescue."

"And you will take me back to Reabon at once?"

"In the morning. Tonight we must seek shelter. The surface of the Azpok swarms with fierce and mighty monsters, which by day seek their dark lairs in the ocean's depths. Night travel in a small boat is extremely dangerous. Hark! I hear the breakers now. The island is not far off."

Steering entirely by the sounds that came to him—for nothing was visible in the pitchy blackness—San Thoy brought the little sailboat through booming breakers which evidently covered a bar or sunken reef, and into comparatively calm water. It was not long after that the keel rasped on a gravelly shore.

Leaping into the shallow water, the pirate dragged the boat high up on the beach. Then he furled the sail, and taking Vernia by the hand, said:

"Come. I will take you to a place where you may spend the night safely. In the morning, I will call for you and take you to Reabon."

"You will be well rewarded," replied Vernia. "I will double the ransom which was offered for me and add to it a thousand kantols of land, and purple of a nobleman for life."

"Your Majesty is generous," said San Thoy, "but then I have cut myself off from my own people, property, and position, in order to effect your rescue."

He led her up a narrow winding path, where leaves, dripping with the night dew, brushed her face and body. Presently they came to a small clearing.

San Thoy fumbled with a latch for a moment, and then opened a door. He released Vernia's hand, and struck a light with the small flame maker which he carried. When he had lighted a torch that hung from a bracket on the wall, Vernia saw that they were in a tiny cabin which contained a sleeping shelf, a crude table, three chairs, some utensils, and a place for cooking beside which fuel was piled.

"I will light the fire for you, that you may dry your clothing," said San Thoy. "Then I will brew kova."

Vernia seated herself on one of the chairs, and watched the broad, greasy back of the pirate as he squatted before the fire. When he had it blazing brightly, he took a kettle and went outside for water. Returning, he dropped in some kova roots which he found on a shelf beside the fireplace, and soon had it boiling. As Vernia watched, she wondered if his intentions were as magnanimous as he pretended, or if he were as perfidious as the words of his commander implied. So far, his impassive features had betrayed nothing. Only time would tell.

Presently, he placed a chair before the fire for her, that she might dry her clothes, and poured her a bowl of steaming kova. While she slowly sipped the hot, stimulating beverage, he tossed off bowl after bowl until the pot was empty and another had been set to brewing. She noticed that with each bowl, the slits in his round eyes became more bestial. San Thoy was drunk.

When the second pot of kova was ready, the pirate offered to refill Vernia's bowl, but she declined. He leered a little as he refilled his own, and it was not long before the second had gone the way of the first. Then San Thoy extracted a kerra pod from his belt pouch, and, breaking it open, emptied the red contents into his toothless mouth.

For a while he mumbled the drug, expectorating thin streams of scarlet juice into the fire from time to time, and muttering drunkenly to himself as they hissed among the hot embers.

Presently he arose, and unclasping a belt which held his tork, scarbo, and knife, hung it on a peg on the wall. Then he stretched his arms and yawned hideously, the red juice trickling from the corners of his flabby mouth, and staining his greasy chin.

"My dear," he said thickly, "it is time to retire. May your humble servant assist you to disrobe?"

With this he lurched unsteadily toward her.

Panic stricken, Vernia jumped up and placed the chair between herself and the advancing pirate.

"Back!" she said. "Go back! Don't you dare touch me!"

"There, there," he said, still advancing. "Do not be frightened. I will not hurt you."

Only the chair and two feet of space separated them now. Suddenly seizing the chair, he hurled it to one side and flung out both arms to grasp her. She leaped back, and his arms embraced empty air. But now she was cornered. She looked longingly at the weapons hanging on the peg, but between her and them was San Thoy.

Half crouching, arms spread, he advanced toward her. Suddenly he sprang like a beast of prey. Then like crushing bands of steel his greasy arms encircled her. His grinning, lecherous features were close to hers, leering down at her.

"Little she-marmelot!" he said. "Think you that you can resist San Thoy, who has subdued a thousand slave-girls?"

She struggled desperately, striking and clawing at the bestial face, squirming and kicking with all her strength, but to no avail.

With a laugh of exultation, he picked her up, and carrying her to the sleeping shelf, flung her down upon it.

A TREACHEROUS SHOAL

THE MONSTER WITH WHICH GRANDON'S fishing boat had collided in the darkness was evidently not of the belligerent type, for it submerged, nearly swamping them, before they attained an even keel.

But they were not yet out of danger. Kantar the Gunner suddenly called to Grandon that the boat had sprung a leak as a result of the collision, and was filling rapidly.

"Then steer for the ship in the center of the squadron, and let us hope that it's the flagship," said Grandon. "I'll row and bail. It's our only chance."

With the strong strokes of Grandon assisting the sail of the swift little vessel, they were able to gain rapidly on the ship

which was at the apex of the wedge-shaped squadron. As they drew near it, Kantar called:

"It is the flagship, Majesty."

"Good. Preserve absolute silence from now on," replied Grandon. "If possible, we must get aboard her without being detected."

Presently they came close enough to hear the sounds of conversation and people moving about. Yet, their boat went unnoticed because the mast lights of the flagship cast little illumination in their direction. The powerful searchlight beams of the ship were directed ahead, as were those of the ships which flanked it on either side.

And they came up under the stern of the pirate vessel without attracting attention. By this time, their boat was half-filled with water, and despite Grandon's bailing was likely to sink at any moment.

Hanging from two pulleys high above them were the two chains with which the rudder was turned from the steersman's cabin in the front of the ship.

"You climb one chain," directed Grandon, "while I go up the other. We are of nearly the same weight, so if we climb at the same time each will counter-balance the other, and the steersman may not notice anything amiss."

Leaping out onto the rudder, Grandon seized the chain on the side opposite them. At the same moment, Kantar grasped the chain next to the boat, and the two went up, hand over hand. Just as Kantar left the little boat, the gunwales went under, and before they had gotten half-way up the chains her masthead disappeared from view. They had reached the flagship just in time.

Together the two men went over the railing, each drawing his scarbo as he did so. A single watchman stood between them, but before he had time even to touch a weapon, a thrust from one side and a cut from the other, laid him low.

The two heaved the body overboard.

"Now," said Grandon grimly, "we'll search the ship."

But scarcely had the words left his mouth when there was a cry from the masthead.

"Enemies on board! Two tall strangers on the after deck. They have slain the guard."

The lookout leveled his tork at them, and a bullet splintered the deck between them. He continued to fire, but fortunately the light was not good. The two men quickly found a temporary refuge by dodging into an empty rear cabin.

"This is a trap," said Grandon. "We can't remain here."

"And yet it would make a good place to take a stand," replied Kantar.

But the decision was not left to them, for the door suddenly burst open, and a yellow pirate leaped in, yelling like a demon. In one hand he grasped a long, heavy knife, and in the other a scarbo which he sought to use.

Grandon quickly silenced him with a thrust to the throat, but his place was immediately taken by two more. Others pressed behind, eager for a chance at the intruders.

Grandon and Kantar, however, were a pair difficult to best with blades of any sort, and it was not long before the floor in front of them was piled high with bodies of their foes. But suddenly a voice called an order from without, and the men, in the thick of the battle, turned and withdrew without a sound, leaving the two alone in the room.

As Kantar turned with a questioning look in his eyes, Grandon saw a small glass globe hurled into the room. Crashing against the wall behind them, it shattered into a thousand tiny fragments. In a moment, Grandon was conscious of an intensely acrid odor. The room whirled. Kantar slid to the floor. The room whirled. Then blackness.

The effects of the gas in the tiny globe were evidently but momentary, for when Grandon once more recovered his senses he was being lifted from the cabin floor by two pirates. The dead bodies of their yellow opponents had been removed, and Kantar was being led out of the room, without his weapons, and with his hands tied behind his back. Grandon moved his arms, and found them securely fastened.

An officer in the uniform of a mojak ordered them brought forward and into a large cabin at the front of the ship. An officer whose uniform proclaimed him Romojak of the fleet was seated at a table, sipping kova.

"Whom have we here, San Thoy?" asked the Romojak, as the two prisoners were brought before him. "It appears that we have captured a royal prisoner, if the taller one rightfully wears the scarlet."

"He does, Excellency," replied San Thoy, "for I recognize him from his description as Grandon of Terra, Torrogo of Reabon."

"Small wonder, then, that our warriors were mowed down like frella grass at harvest," said the Romojak. "Few men can face him with a scarbo and live!" He arose and bowed to Grandon. "I am honored, Your Majesty," he said, "by your unexpected visit to my humble ship. Now that you are here, I trust that you and your warrior will remain as our guests."

"Who are you, you yellow knave?" demanded Grandon, "and what have you done with the Torroga of Reabon?"

The Romojak returned his haughty look.

"I am Thid Yet, Romojak of the Fleets of Huitsen," he answered with exaggerated deference, "and Your Imperial Majesty, of the Torroga of Reabon, I know absolutely nothing. If you seek her here, you have been misinformed as to her whereabouts."

"I see that you are as skilled in the art of lying as in that of abduction," said Grandon. "But listen to me. You Huitsenni have gone unpunished for many generations. You shall not escape this time. Whereas Huitsen is now an unsavory word, when the fleets of Reabon have done, it will be but a stinking memory—except on one condition."

"Your threats do not impress me, but," said Thid Yet, "I will inquire the condition out of courtesy."

"That you immediately place my wife, my warrior, and myself safely back on Reabonian soil."

"I can only repeat," said Thid Yet, "that I know nothing whatever of the whereabouts of your wife. As for placing you and your soldier safely back upon Reabonian soil, we shall be delighted to do this for you. This, however, would entail some expense and no slight danger to us, and as you came aboard our ship unbidden, we feel that it is only fair that we should be reimbursed to the slight extent of, say, a hundred thousand white slaves, young and strong, and a million keds of gold."

"What! You asked the price of an empire to set us ashore," exclaimed Kantar, "and a hundred thousand slaves besides?"

"One does not set a Torrogo of Reabon ashore every day," replied Thid Yet with a toothless grin.

"Set my wife ashore with us, unharmed, and I will pay you two million keds of gold," said Grandon. "The second million is in lieu of the hundred thousand slaves, a commodity in which I do not care to traffic."

Thid Yet grinned again.

"I'm afraid I shall have to ask you to be our guests for an indefinite period of time. Show them to the guest chambers, San Thoy."

Grandon and Kantar were hustled out of the cabin, and along the deck to a hatchway leading into the hold. Down this they were lowered like freight, and each was seized by a grinning yellow buccaneer.

"To the guest chambers," ordered San Thoy, and strolled away.

The two new guards hustled the prisoners along a dimly lighted passageway, threw them with their hands still bound behind them, into a small, evil-smelling room, and closed and bolted the door after them.

Flung violently into the room, Grandon's head collided with one of the stalwart ribs which braced the ship's sides, dazing him momentarily. He was brought back to full consciousness by Kantar calling to him.

"Are you hurt, Majesty?"

"A bit dazed," replied Grandon, "but I'll be all right in a moment. And you?"

"Only bruised a little."

"Then come over here and let me see if I can loose your bonds. We must get out some way and search the ship."

Soon the two men were seated on the damp, filthy floor, back to back, and Grandon was working desperately at the bonds which held Kantar's wrists. Opening the tight knots which the yellow sailors had tied would have been no easy task even with his eyes to guide him and his hands free. But he worked patiently, doggedly, until at length a knot was opened. Soon a second yielded, and Kantar, with an exclamation of relief, chafed his numbed wrists for a moment, then swiftly began the task of releasing Grandon's hands. This took less time, as the gunner could work with his hands in front of him.

When Grandon had restored the circulation to his wrists, he tried the door. It was of thick planking, and bolted so tightly that he could not budge it, but the planks, after having been fastened together, had evidently shrunk a little, as there were narrow cracks between them and on each side between door and frame.

Kantar examined the lock, and said:

"If I only had a knife I could lift that bolt and open the door."

"Unfortunately," replied Grandon, "we have no knife, nor have we anything which will answer for one. It is possible, however, that we can get the guard to open the door."

"How?"

"By pretending that one of us is killing the other. Dead prisoners are of no use to the Huitsenni. Let us first make believe that we are quarreling. You will lie on the floor with your hands behind you as if they were still bound. First we will quarrel, then you will thump on the floor with your hands and shout that you are being kicked to death. Let us try it."

Kantar accordingly took his place on the floor, while Grandon stood where he would be behind the door when it was opened, and looked out into the hallway. As soon as the guard approached, he raised his voice and began abusing Kantar with choice patoan epithets, accusing him of having gotten him into the scrape, and threatening to kill him then and there.

Kantar replied, apparently pleading for clemency, and Grandon saw the guard pause outside and listen with a broad grin on his face. But when Kantar began thumping on the floor with the palm of his hand and shouting that he was being killed, the expression on the guard's face grew serious, and he quickly opened the door.

Scarcely had he stepped inside when Grandon sprang. Seizing him from behind with a strangle hold, he jerked the guard backward, shutting off his wind. At the same time, Kantar stood up and quietly deprived him of his weapons.

"Close the door, Kantar, until we talk to this fellow," said Grandon.

"Now," said the Earth-man, when the gunner had complied, "we want to know where her Majesty of Reabon is imprisoned. If you go with us quietly and show us the place, you will live. If not, you will die. Nod your head if you agree."

The guard, whose voice was completely shut off, nodded weakly, and Grandon loosened the hold on his throat, permitting him to breathe once more.

"Give me the scarbo, Kantar," said Grandon, "and retain the tork and knife for yourself. Keep a good hold on the fellow's harness, and do not hesitate to use your knife if he makes one move to betray us."

"In such an event I will use it with great pleasure, Majesty," said Kantar grimly.

Carefully opening the door, Grandon peered out. There was no one in the hallway.

"Where is the other guard?" he asked their captive.

"He patrols the forward corridor, Majesty," replied the guard respectfully. "It is connected with this one by two smaller corridors that branch around the central hatchway. He does not come into this corridor except at my call."

"Good. Then lead us to the Princess by the safest route. And remember, if we are discovered through fault of yours, you die."

Thus admonished, the thoroughly cowed guard led them to a ladder which descended into the corridor from the side, and with Kantar gripping his harness with one hand and his keen knife with the other, softly ascended. They came on deck near the stern and quietly made their way forward, keeping in the shadow of the cabins in order not to be observed by the lookout at the masthead.

They had covered about half the distance to the forward cabin for which they were headed, when Grandon suddenly noticed a short, thick-set individual who had apparently just emerged from one of the cabins, carrying a bundle in his arms and hurrying toward one of the four small boats slung on this side of the craft.

After placing the bundle, which was nearly as long as himself, in the boat, the fellow, whom Grandon now recognized as San Thoy, climbed in himself and rapidly lowered the little craft to the water by means of the two ropes which passed through pulleys suspended on davits. He and his two companions flattened themselves against the cabin wall until the small boat had disappeared from view over the rail—then went forward once more.

Presently their conductor stopped before a door and whispered:

"This is her cabin."

While Kantar watched their guide, Grandon tried the cabin door, and finding it unlocked, stepped inside. By the rays of the tiny overhead light which illuminated the little room, he could see at a glance that it was deserted. His brow clouded, and it would have gone ill with the yellow man who had led him to this cabin had he not noticed something on the floor which glinted in the light. He picked it up, and recognized it instantly as one of the jewels from Vernia's coiffure.

Stepping out of the cabin once more, he seized the guard's shoulder in a grip of iron.

"She is not here," he said, sternly, and raised his scarbo as if he were about to lay the fellow's head open.

"Spare me, Majesty," implored the yellow man. "This was her cabin. I swear it."

"Then how do you explain her absence: Speak quickly if you would live?"

"I see it all, Majesty," said the guard suddenly. "We are too late!"

"Too late? What do you mean?"

"Your Majesty saw San Thoy with the bundle—San Thoy the debauched—who spends all his earnings for beautiful slave girls. He would dare much to possess the most beautiful woman of Zorovia."

"Then we will follow San Thoy," said Grandon, "and you will go with us. Perhaps you can give us an idea where he has gone. To the nearest boat, Kantar, and use your tork if the lookout sees us."

"He will not see us, Majesty," said the guard. "Of that I am sure, as San Thoy must have seen to it that he is either drugged or dead—probably the latter."

True to the prediction of the yellow guard, there was no alarm from the masthead, nor from any other part of the ship as they lowered the boat to the water and cast off. It was equipped with a small sail, which they raised as soon as the fleet was far enough away to make it improbable that it would be observed.

"Now," said Grandon, "which way do you think San Thoy sailed?"

"I can not be sure," replied the guard, "But the nearest land is the Island of the Valkars. It has a small cove, accessible in a small boat, where the Huitsenni often stop for fresh water, and where they have erected a small but strong shelter into which they may retire if surprised by a large force of the terrible inhabitants of the place. It may be that he has gone to this shelter for the night, intending to embark for some safer place tomorrow."

"Can you guide us to it?"

"I can but try, Majesty. I am no navigator like San Thoy, who can probably win safely across the shoals into the cove without even the aid of a light. But the island is a large one, and I know the general direction. If I steer properly we should reach some part of its rugged coast in a short time."

"Then," said Kantar, grimly, "see that you steer properly if you would live to see tomorrow's light."

The mast lights of the fleet were twinkling faintly in the distance as the yellow man took the tiller, and swinging it around set his course. After taking the precaution of securing his prisoner's ankles with a piece of rope, Kantar sat down a short distance ahead of him and managed to sail, while Grandon kept watch in the front of the craft.

They had not traveled far before the boom of breakers sounded ahead.

"There is the Island of the Valkars," said the prisoner, "But I know not how to find the cove. If we should try to land anywhere else we would be almost certain either to be dashed to pieces on the rugged shore or sunk by the jagged teeth of one of the many hidden reefs which circle the island.

If we do land in safety, we may be set upon in the darkness
by the Valkars, and carried away to be devoured."

"What are these Valkars?" asked Grandon.

"I, who have sailed every ocean of Zorovia, have never
seen creatures more horrible." said the yellow man. "En-
dowed with human intelligence, they manufacture and use
weapons and implements of metal, yet they are not human, nor
even mammalian. They are amphibians. Twice we fought them
off when we landed for water. I was a member of the landing
party. Although we outnumbered them each time, we lost
several men in each engagement. Some were torn to pieces
and devoured before our eyes. Others of our slain and wounded were carried away.

"But that was not all. After our ship had left the island
following the first engagement with the Valkars, those of our
men who had been stabbed, cut, bitten, or scratched in the
battle, though ever so slightly, began dying horrible deaths.
Our mojak, who was wiser than most, had one of our Valkar
prisoners slain, and according to an ancient custom, ordered
every man who had received so much as a scratch to either
drink a drop of its blood or eat a mouthful of its flesh. The
men who complied with this order in time lived, but we did
not know the reason until later.

"We took two captured Valkars to Huitsen, where they were
examined by our most learned scientists. They found that these
creatures secrete a venom from glands in their mouths, and
before going into battle, smear their weapons and claws with
it. In their blood, however, is a substance, a small quantity
of which counteracts the effect of the venom. Because they
were venomous, they apparently thought we were, also, and it
was evidently for that reason that some of our men were torn
to pieces on the battlefield and their fragments distributed
among and devoured by our enemies."

While they were talking, Grandon had been straining his
eyes into the darkness before them. Suddenly he exclaimed:

"I see a light dead ahead!"

"Then I have steered better than I could have hoped," said the yellow pirate, "for it must be the light from the cabin in the cove. We will be there shortly if we can pass through the shoals unscathed."

He set his course dead ahead, asking Grandon to watch the light and direct him, as he was unable to see it from the stern on account of the sail. This Grandon did, and was greatly mystified as he watched, for although the light had seemed to be not more than a mile away when he first saw it, and they continued to sail swiftly toward it, it did not increase in brightness or apparent nearness. It seemed to have an unnatural, phosphorescent gleam, also, that would scarcely be expected to come from a cabin light.

The breakers roared louder and louder as they progressed. Suddenly their hull glanced from a submerged rock, scraped a second, and smashed, head on, into a third. There was a rendering crash as the little craft swung half around, buffeted by the waves for a moment before a huge roller engulfed her.

Just beyond the treacherous shoal, two men struggled desperately in the boiling, seething water, in an effort to reach the shore. But the third had gone down, never to rise again.

C H A P T E R V

THE TOAD PEOPLE

PANTING HEAVILY FROM HIS EXERTIONS, San Thoy leaned gloatingly over Vernia, lying where he had thrown her on the sleeping shelf. But his look of exhultation suddenly turned to one of amazement. She had drawn back her foot and planted the heel in his solar plexus with such force that he staggered back across the little cabin, gasping for breath, until tripped by a chair and thrown to the floor.

She did not wait to see what he would do, but sprang to her feet and dashed out of the cabin. But San Thoy was unusually agile for a man of his rotund build, and she had not taken ten steps beyond the door of the cabin before he was up and after her.

Bounding off into the darkness with no sense of direction, and no thought in mind save that of escaping the pursuer from whose clutches she had just broken, Vernia suddenly became conscious of many pairs of gleaming eyes. Reflecting the light from the open door, they seemed to be looking at her from the surrounding darkness.

With a little scream of terror, she halted in her tracks, and San Thoy, uttering a cry of triumph, leaped forward to recapture her. But a keen barbed hook on the end of a long pole suddenly shot out from the darkness at his right, and as it pierced his shoulder, his shout of triumph became an agonized shriek. It jerked him backward, so that his feet flew from under him and he sat down with considerable violence.

At the same time, a heavy body came hurtling through the air and landed on two webbed feet in front of Vernia. It was about the height of a large man, and stood erect on two bowed legs with its toes turned so far outward that the two feet, with the heels together, were almost in line. The body was thick and heavy, and covered with scales in front. On the back and sides these scales were interspersed with huge bumps, which were also in evidence on the backs of the upper and lower limbs and on the head. The mouth was an enormous slit which reached nearly from ear to ear, armed with saw-like ridges of jaw bone in lieu of teeth. The eyes were large and set in bony sockets that protruded above the cheek bones. Like the feet, the hands were webbed and armed with sharp claws.

Thus the creature which stood before Vernia might have been nothing more than a very large and ferocious looking toad. But the fact that it carried weapons—a pole with a hook on the end like that which had impaled San Thoy, and a mace with a curved bill which hung by a thong from its wrist—and that it wore a belt in which a large knife was thrust, made it evident that this was no common toad. It was infinitely more formidable and terrible than a creature with the mind as well as the body of a toad could have been. Its use of weapons was

evidence of an intelligence which was at least equal to that of
the most primitive men.

The creature uttered a hoarse croaking cry, and threw a cold
scaly arm around Vernia's waist, slinging her over its shoulder
with an ease that bespoke enormous strength. After struggling
desperately for a moment, she realized the futility of attempting
to pit her strength against that of the monster, and lay still.

As if it had been a signal or a call, the sound made by her
captor brought a score of the creatures circling around them,
all armed like the first. The beast that had captured San Thoy
unhooked him without any attention to his cries of anguish,
and threw him, writhing and moaning, over its warty shoulder.
Then the entire group, led by Vernia's captor, marched away.

As it was pitch dark after they left the vicinity of the lighted
cabin, Vernia was unable to see where they were going. She
judged, however, from the movements of her captor, that they
were traversing some exceedingly rugged country. Presently,
this gave way to marshy lowlands, through which the toad
men leaped and splashed, then to firmer ground covered with
tall, coarse grass that brushed against Vernia as she was
carried through it.

When the coming of the dawn made it possible for her to
see, she found herself in the midst of a city of low, moss-covered
mounds. In each of these mounds, a hole on the ground level,
about three feet in diameter, served as a doorway, and from
most of the doorways the huge inquiring eyes of the inhabitants
peeped cautiously out at the prisoners as they were being
brought in.

Many of the other creatures which were moving about the
place paused to stare at Vernia, as if they had never seen any
one of her race before. San Thoy, it appeared, was of a race
which they had previously seen. At least he did not attract
nearly so much attention.

A shallow, sluggish stream with muddy bottom meandered
through the center of the village, and seated on its banks or

"*Then the entire group, led by Vernia's captor, marched away.*"

Chapter V.

partly submerged in its leisurely flowing water, a number of
the creatures dozed languidly.

The adult creatures on the bank and in the water, Vernia
noticed, were all females—smaller than the males, and if possible more hideous. But hopping and crawling around them,
and swimming in the muddy water, were hundreds of young-
sters, apparently newly hatched, and none over eight inches tall.

Her captor chancing to walk quite near the bank with her,
Vernia saw, with some surprise, that the placidly dozing females were there for a purpose, that of hatching their young;
for she saw one of the large lumps on the back of the nearest
female burst open, and an infant, after tumbling out into the
mud, made straight for the water and dive in. Its mother
paid no attention whatever to the incident, nor did she so much
as turn to look at her offspring. Several other lumps on her
back had already burst open, and she was waiting for the rest
to do the same.

Presently her captor left the bank of the stream, and after
threading many pathways between the numerous mounds,
stopped before a mound which was much larger than any of
the others and appeared to be in the very heart of the city. It
had a number of entrances, but her captor chose the largest,
and stopping, walked through it into a large, dome like room
which was lighted by a peculiar, phosphorescent radiance that
gave everything a ghastly greenish tint. This peculiar light
came from immense writhing glowworms suspended on chains
overhead. The air of the place was filled with a musty stench,
similar to that which Vernia had noticed outside, but here
so strong as to be almost overpowering.

Her captor swung her down from his warty shoulders, and
set her on her feet. Then she was whirled around to face a
creature much more repulsive looking than the one that had
captured her. It was squatting on the slimy cap of a gray
toadstool set against the rear wall, staring at her with its gog-
gling, gold-rimmed eyes. Its scaly hide draped its body in

wrinkled folds, and there was about it a look of dried-up emaciation, as if it were very old and partly mummified.

One taloned hand held a huge mace with a curved bill. The other toyed with the hilt of a long, curved knife that hung from a massive chain girdling the monster's middle.

On either side of the fungoid throne occupied by the hideous creature was a yellow man of Huitsen, standing with folded arms in the attitude of a slave. These two pirates, captives of the toad people and evidently in attendance to the repulsive thing which seemed to be in authority, were quite filthy, and clothed in a few tattered rags which had once been garments. Both leered at the beautiful captive with their cat-like eyes, and grinned toothlessly.

After staring at her for fully five minutes, the squat monster on the toadstool rolled its gold rimmed eyes toward the yellow man who stood at its right, and emitted a rapid succession of hoarse, booming croaks.

Much to Vernia's surprise the man replied in a human approximation of the same sounds—evidently the language of the toad people. Then he addressed Vernia: "His Majesty wishes to know your name, and whence you came," he said in patoa.

Vernia raised her eyebrows: "His Majesty! Do you refer to that croaking monster?"

"I refer to Grunk, Rogo of the Valkars. On this island his wish is law. It will be wise for you to answer his question."

"Tell him that I am Vernia, Torroga of Reabon," she directed, "and that he will be richly rewarded if I am returned, unharmed, to my people."

For several minutes the toad ruler and the yellow man carried on a croaking conversation. Then the latter addressed Vernia once more.

"His Majesty knows nothing of rewards, nor is he concerned with them," said he. "It was difficult for me to convey the idea to him in the Valkar language, and even then it did not impress him. He is interested in you for one reason, and that is because you are the first human female his warriors have ever captured. A number of the Huitsenni, who stop at this island for fresh water, have been captured and enslaved from time to time by the toad people. As we are more skillful than they in mining and smelting metals and the manufacture of weapons, tools, chains, and ornaments, they set us at these tasks. They recognize, also that some of us have superior cunning, I, Hui Sen, and my brother, Lui Sen, are retained for that reason as counsellors for the rogo. We try to do our work well, for as long as we prove useful we will be kept alive. But if our work displeases Grunk, we will either be killed and eaten by the Valkars or fed to Sistabez."

"And who is Sistabez?"

"The deity of the Toad People. They think him a god, though he is only a snake—an immense serpent who must be at least a thousand years old, for he has outlived many generation of Valkars. As far back as Valkar tradition goes, Sistabez has lived in his cave in the mountainside, emerging at regular intervals when hungry. At such times living sacrifices are fed to him in order to keep him from raiding the village, which he has done several times when sacrifices were not brought promptly.

"Sometimes he devours but one victim. At other times he is not satisfied with less than three or four. When he is seen emerging from his cave, guards sound the alarm, and a victim is chained to a stake in his path. A second victim is chained farther down the pathway, and a third still farther. He may devour only the first, or perhaps the first and second, but sometimes he comes on and devours the third. If he turns back to his cave then, all is well. If not, a fourth victim is chained in his pathway. Never has he been known to devour more than four victims at one meal, but woe be to the Valkars if he becomes angry, for then he will wantonly slay hundreds before returning to his lair."

Once more, Hui Sen turned and deferentially addressed Grunk in the croaking language. For some time the Rogo of the Valkars made no reply, but continued to stare at Vernia with his round, gold-rimmed eyes. Then, apparently having come to some decision, he croaked an order to the yellow slave.

"His Majesty," said Hui Sen, "has decided to retain you alive that you may serve the purpose for which females were created, and thus multiply the number of his slaves. Later, he will make some mental tests among the slaves, to determine who shall be your mate."

Up to this moment, Vernia had desired to live, hoping in the face of despair that she might some day be restored to Grandon. But as the significance of Hui Sen's words sank into her brain, her one desire was for speedy death. The hilt of her captor's knife projected invitingly before her. Suddenly turning, she whipped it from the sheath and drew it back to plunge it into her bosom. But Lui Sen, standing beside the throne, while less talkative than his brother, was more observing, and the first to perceive her intention. With a cat-like spring he alighted in front of her, seized her wrist, and wrenched the knife from her grasp. Then the Rogo croaked an order, and Vernia's captor dragged her out of the hut.

She was led through the village of moss covered mounds, toward a large mound in the midst of an extensive enclosure, surrounded by a paling of metal bars and guarded by armed Valkars. After exchanging croaks with her conductor, one of the guards opened a gate, and she was pushed into the enclosure. Here, several hundred Huitsenni slaves were at work, forging, sharpening, and polishing weapons for their batrachian masters under the supervision of armed Valkar overseers. The forges were hollowed stones in which were beds of live coals. The bellows were the lungs of huge Valkars, who blew through reed tubes which entered holes in the bottoms of the forges. The anvils were large, rounded stones, at which the yellow workers squatted as they hammered out hooks, mace heads, and knife blades.

The place was a bedlam—the clanking of metal, the roar of flames, the croaks of the overseers, and the chatter of the slaves. The floor of the enclosure was littered with filth and everywhere spattered with red kerra juice. The Valkars, though they did not use the narcotic themselves, evidently believed that it made their human slaves more efficient, and kept them well supplied with the pods containing the red spores, which they mumbled from morning to night, and spat unbelievable quantities of reddened saliva all about them.

Other workers were sharpening the knife blades, hook points and barbs, and mace bills, with rough stones, and still others were polishing them with sand. The metal parts then went to the assemblers, where the knives and maces were fitted with wooden handles, and the hooks with long shafts.

Sickened by the squalor of the place, and overwhelmed with horror at thought of the fate which Grunk, Rogo of the Valkars, planned for her, Vernia shrank back against the bars of the enclosure. The yellow ex-pirates seemed fully aware of Grunk's intentions with regard to her, and raised lascivious eyes from their work to drink in her beauty, the while they bandied coarse jests, and speculated as to who would be the lucky slave to draw this prize of feminine pulchritude for whom mighty emperors had contended in vain.

Quite near her, a group of Huitsenni was assembling knives, tossing them into a central pile when finished. With one of these in her possession, she could swiftly defeat the purpose of Grunk. It was only a few steps to the pile. Would they divine her purpose?

She decided that a circuitous route would be the least likely to make them suspicious. So she set off first in the opposite direction, pausing to watch various groups of workers as if greatly interested in what they were doing. The coarse jokes of each group subsided as she drew near each in turn. They were more than a little awed by the imminence of the Torroga of Reabon. And there were a number of egotistical creatures among them who strove to impress her with attempts at dignity and gentle bearing.

Last of all, she approached the group of workers surrounding the rapidly mounting pile of knives. Casually, she picked up one of the finished weapons as if to examine it. With a swift movement, she raised it aloft, poised above her breast.

A greasy yellow hand reached over her shoulder—seized her wrist and shook the knife from her grasp. Then a coarse laugh grated in her ear.

She spun around to face the filthy and ragged Hui Sen. Evidently he had been stealthily following her for some time.

"Come," he grinned toothlessly, retaining a tight grip on her wrist. "From now on you belong to me, for I am the Rogo's choice."

C H A P T E R VI

THE DECEPTIVE LIGHT

AS GRANDON STRUGGLED IN THE SEETH-
ing water, he strove to look about him for some sign of Kantar
the Gunner. But save for that phosphorescent luminescence
which had lured them onto the rocks, all was blackness.

"Kantar!" he shouted. "Kantar! Where are you?"

A big roller caught him unawares. Part of it he inhaled.
Strangling and choking, he endeavored to rid his tortured
lungs of the smarting brine. All the time he was being
carried swiftly toward that deceptive phosphoresence. The
roar of the breakers grew deafening. He realized, then, that if
Kantar had been within fifty feet of him when he shouted,
he probably would not have heard his cry.

Presently his hands struck a sloping ledge of sharp coral. He drew himself up onto it, and stood erect. But a giant comber knocked him flat, cutting his hands, face, and body on the jagged coral. After that he crawled forward painfully. At length the coral was replaced by rugged bits of stone, and finally by a sharply slanting beach where jointed saw-toothed reeds grew among out-croppings of volcanic rock. For some time he rested on a slab of water-worn lava, panting heavily from his exertions. His cuts and scratches were rendered doubly painful by the salt water.

Presently he stood up. The phosphorescent light was not more than five hundred feet away, and it seemed to be slowly moving toward him in a rather erratic fashion. It lit up the waving reeds and brakish pools with a pale greenish white luminescence. As he watched, it stopped behind a clump of tall reeds.

Suddenly, between himself and the light he saw a human form sloshing through the pools. There was something familiar about the bedraggled figure, and he recognized the gunner.

"Kantar!" he shouted, running forward.

The figure splashed onward, unable to hear him because of the roar of the breakers. At a distance of a few feet he again shouted: "Kantar!" at the top of his voice.

The gunner turned.

"Majesty!" he exclaimed. "I had thought you drowned with that yellow pirate. Praise Thorth, you are alive!"

"We must find that hut of the Huitsenni, quickly," said Grandon as he came up. "Have you any idea where to look for it?"

"Our guide said there would be a light," replied Kantar. "I was about to investigate this one."

"I saw it moving a moment ago," said Grandon. "I doubt that the cabin would be built in a salt marsh, or that a light in it would move about as this one has. Perhaps it is a light carried by one of the creatures the pirates called 'Valkars.' But it will do no harm to investigate."

Cautiously they crept forward through the marsh, bending down below the level of the waving reeds so that they would not be seen. Presently Kantar laid a hand on Grandon's arm, and exclaimed: "I see it, Majesty! Why, it's an enormous worm!"

Looking through the place where the gunner had parted the reeds, the Earthman saw a fat, grub-like creature about five feet in length. Its entire body glowed with a greenish white light. Leisurely it moved among the reeds, browsing on the water plants that grew in the bottoms of the brakish pools.

Disturbed at its feeding by the sound, the creature reared its luminous head and spied them. Arching its neck, it gnashed its mandibles threatingly.

"I wonder if that thing would shine as brightly dead as alive," said Grandon. "If so, it would be useful to us."

For answer, Kantar elevated the muzzle of his tork, and pressing the firing button, deftly sprayed a line of the needle-like projectiles across the luminous throat.

Cut off as cleanly as if by a sword blade in the hands of an expert, the head fell from the body, which immediately began writhing and thrashing about in the rushes and shallow water.

"Neatly done, Gunner," commented Grandon. "Why the thing appears to be shining more than ever! Now for a couple of torches."

So saying, he whipped out his scarbo, and advancing to where the headless thing squirmed and floundered in the reeds, cut off two sections, each about a foot in length. Then, with two sharpened reeds which he thrust into the sections for handles, he made a pair of torches, each of which was capable of lighting up the terrain for at least fifty feet in every direction.

Grandon passed one torch to Kantar, and holding the other above his head, set off along the shore line in the hope of coming upon the cabin which their yellow prisoner had described, and where he believed they would find Vernia in the power of the unscrupulous San Thoy. But though they traveled as swiftly as the rugged character of the shore line would permit for the rest of the night, morning dawned without their having reached their objective.

With his scarbo, Grandon speared a large, spiny fish, left by the ebbing tide in a small pool. They cooked a portion of it over a fire of dry reeds ignited by Grandon's flame maker. It was tough, bony, and rather tasteless, but a welcome meal, nevertheless, to the two hungry men.

As soon as they had breakfast, they set off once more along the shore line. Shortly thereafter, the character of the terrain underwent a decided change. The ground sloped upward, and instead of marsh behind them, there was now a belt of fern forest. And the flat beach gave way to rugged rock ledges, then towering cliffs, clothed to their very edges with tree ferns, bush ferns, and many creeping and climbing varieties, as well as a few species of cycads and other primitive types. Here there grew in abundance the large Zorovian water ferns, the ribs of which contain water, clear, cold, and sweet as any that may be found on Venus. They paused, and broke off enough fronds to assuage their thirst and fill their canteens. Then they pressed onward.

Soon they came, quite unexpectedly, upon a small natural harbor. The entrance was a narrow channel which zig-zagged between tall cliffs, and the little inland bay, protected from wind and waves by this natural barrier, was as smooth as glass.

"This must be the cove described by our prisoner," said Grandon, excitedly. "The cabin should not be far off."

"I see it, Majesty," cried the sharp-eyed gunner, "over near the center of the bay. It's partly hidden by the tree ferns."

"Sure enough! Come on."

Grandon led the way at so swift a pace now, that the tired gunner was sorely put to it to keep up with him. As they neared the cabin, the sight of the small boat which had been

left there by San Thoy caused Grandon to hurry faster than
ever, for he now felt positive that he should find Vernia and her
captor in the cabin. But within less than a hundred feet of
the cabin, he stopped suddenly.

"We must approach with caution, Gunner," he said. "The
yellow beast is probably armed with a tork, and it wouldn't
be healthy for us if he saw or heard us coming. Better go in
from two different directions, too, so if he gets one of us the
other will have a chance at him."

They separated accordingly, and circling the cabin, crept
cautiously up to it from opposite directions. The first to reach
the front of the little building, Grandon saw the door standing
wide open. With drawn scarbo, he leaped through, then
stopped in amazement, for a single glance around the room
told him that it was deserted.

The gunner was only a few steps behind Grandon.

"Gone?" he asked.

"So it seems. But where?"

Hanging on a peg at one side of the room was a belt containing a scarbo, tork, and knife. Grandon's shoulder struck
the hanging scarbo, and it clanked against the tork.

"What's this?" he exclaimed, lifting the belt from the peg.
"Why, these are the weapons of San Thoy! His name is en-
graved on the belt buckle in patoan characters."

"I judge that he would not willingly have left without them."

"No, not willingly."

"Then who could have carried them off, and what has become of Her Majesty, your wife?"

"Who but the Valkars, those toad-like monsters that our
prisoner described. We must find the trail. I'll take San
Thoy's weapons and give the other scarbo to you. Then we'll
both be fully armed."

Soon Grandon, who had learned his woodcraft from the
Fighting Traveks, his fierce mountaineer subjects of Uxpo,
and learned it well, discovered blood spots about a hundred

feet from the door of the hut. And in the soft leaf mold were the small footprints of a woman, the large prints of a man, and the still larger tracks of webbed and clawed feet. Kantar who was born and bred in the mountain fastnesses of Uxpo, read the signs as quickly as did the Earth-man.

"She ran out here to escape the yellow pirate," he said.

"And both were carried off by the Valkars," finished Grandon. "Blood was spilled. I trust that it was not hers."

"It starts at the point where San Thoy was lifted off his feet."

"True enough. Let us hope for the best. And now to the trail."

It was not difficult for the two trained woodsmen to follow the well-marked trail of the toad people. It led them through the belt of thick fern forest that fringed the shore, and across a range of rugged and sparsely wooded hills, into a gloomy and treacherous swamp. Here Grandon, at almost the first step, sank into a quagmire up to his chin. It would speedily have closed over his head, had not Kantar been there to extend a helping hand. Even then, it was with the greatest difficulty that the gunner succeeded in drawing him out of the clinging, sticky mess.

After this misadventure, Grandon took more care where he stepped, quickly learning that a piece of ground which was safe for a web-footed Valkar might be extremely perilous for a man. He chafed at the delay occasioned by the necessity of testing each bit of soil before stepping on it, but was constrained by the obvious verity that if he did not travel with caution his travels would soon be terminated.

Nor was the treacherous footing the sole menace the swamp held for the two. They were constantly compelled to be on the lookout for venomous snakes which crawled across their pathway, and tremendous whistling serpents that dangled from tree limbs, waiting for unsuspecting victims on which to drop, then crush the life out of them with their immense muscular coils. In addition, they were compelled to avoid the huge saurians which made the morass their habitation. Some of these were herbivores, and harmless unless disturbed, but others, the mighty carnivores which fed on these and any other smaller bits of flesh that came their way, would make short work of them if they suspected this pair of tender, two-legged animals was crossing their feeding ground. Annoying, too, were the constant attacks of biting and stinging insect pests which buzzed in thick clouds about them.

Both men heaved a sigh of relief when they presently reached higher and drier ground, for though the tall grass through which the path wound might harbor even more dangerous enemies than they had seen in the swamp, they were at least sure of their footing, and soon left the bulk of their insect tormentors behind.

They had traveled about a mile into this grassy savanna, when Grandon suddenly caught his companion by the arm.

"Quiet!" he said. "I hear something coming!"

Unmistakably there came to the ears of both the sound of someone or something speeding through the tall grass, then a shriek of pain or terror, and a hoarse booming croak.

"Come on," cried Grandon. "It sounds like a human being attacked by some fierce beast."

They had only taken a few steps in the direction of the sounds when there hove into view, running for his life, a short, bandy-legged yellow man. Although Grandon and Kantar had never seen a Valkar, both instantly identified the hideous, warty creature which followed in swift pursuit, from the description their former prisoner had given them. It was rapidly shortening the distance between itself and its shrieking quarry, and the long pole it carried, tipped with a barbed hook, was extended to transfix its victim.

Kantar elevated the muzzle of his tork.

"Don't shoot," warned Grandon. "The sound may betray us, and bring a horde of these creatures. You grab the yellow man, and I'll take the Valkar."

Whipping out his scarbo, the Earth-man accordingly crouched in the grass at one side of the part, while Kantar, similarly
armed, concealed himself on the other side.

Just as he came opposite them, the fugitive was caught by
the barbed hook. He uttered an agonized shriek as it pierced
his arm. But before his pursuer could jerk him backward,
Kantar's scarbo had cut through the shaft. And Grandon,
blade in hand, had leaped at the Valkar.

Although he was taken by surprise, the toad man was re-
markably quick. Dropping his useless shaft, he snatched his
long knife from his belt, and raised it to parry the cut which
Grandon aimed at his head. It turned the blade of the scarbo
so that, in descending it only cut a small slice from the scaly
shoulder. At the same instant, with lightning quickness, he
struck the Earth-man with the mace in his left hand.

The blow took Grandon by surprise, and the hooked bill
bit into his right shoulder, which he had instinctively raised
to protect his face, inflicting a painful wound. With a croak
of triumph, the monster jerked the Earth-man toward him, in-
tent on finishing him with the knife. But at that instant, Grandon drew back his lowered scarbo, then thrust upward with
all his might. The blade, driven with terrific force, entered
the silver-gray throat, and passing upward through the head,
came out between the bulging eyes. With a hoarse death
croak, the Valkar sank to the ground, kicking convulsively.

Kantar came running up, dragging his yellow prisoner, from
whose arm he had extracted the barbed hook.

"Why, you are bleeding, Majesty!" he exclaimed.

"Only a flesh wound," replied Grandon. "I'll be all right."

The gunner twisted the small cup from the top of his kova
flask, and held it to the bleeding throat of the dying Valkar.
In an instant it was filled with blood. He stood up and proffered the cup to Grandon.

"You must drink this quickly, Majesty," he said, " or your
wound may prove fatal."

"What's the matter with you?" demand the Earthman. "Have you gone crazy?"

"Drink quickly, I beg of you. It is the only antidote for the venom with which these monsters smear their weapons."

"Right. I had forgotten what our prisoner told us." He took the proffered cup, and with a wry face, drained it. The wounded yellow man, whose wrist Kantar was holding, had meanwhile crouched down, and was lapping at the bleeding throat of the Valkar.

"Let me bind your wound, Majesty," said the gunner.

"No. It is not large, and will close itself. Meanwhile, let us examine the prisoner." He glared at the diminutive yellow man, who now stood with bowed head, his wrist still clutched by Kantar. "Are you San Thoy?" he asked.

"No, Majesty," replied the prisoner, who, noting the scarlet of Grandon's attire was aware that he stood before royalty. "San Thoy is a great mojak, while I, as your Majesty may see by the remains of my raiment, am only a common sailor."

"Your name, sailor."

"So Lan, Majesty, late of the ship, Sagana, of the Imperial Navy of Huitsen. I was captured by the Valkars three endirs ago with a dozen of my mates when we were sent ashore for fresh water. Today I escaped from the prison compound, but this Valkar hunter saw me, and would have slain me or taken me back a prisoner had not you come up."

"Saw you ought of San Thoy?"

"He, and a beautiful white princess, who some say was Vernia of Reabon, were brought in prisoners this morning."

"Where are they now?"

"The white princess was brought to the slave compound shortly before I made my escape. It was the attention she attracted, both from the slaves and the Valkars, which made it possible for me to get away undetected."

"And what do these Valkars intend to do with her? Hold her for ransom?"

"No, Majesty. They care nothing for money, or any other things of great worth. But I heard that Grunk, their Rogo, who has never before captured a human female, planned to keep her for the purpose of breeding a race of slaves."

"Enough! Lead us at once to this compound. Perform your task faithfully, take me to a spot where I can set eyes on my wife, and you will be permitted to escape again. But remember, one sign of treachery, and you die."

"Your wife! Then you are the famed Grandon of Terra, the hero from the planet Mignor, who won the most beautiful woman on Zorovia!" He dropped to his knees, and with both hands extended, palms downward, pressed his forehead to the ground. "I do homage to so mighty a swordsman and so famed a ruler," he muttered.

"Up, and cease this mummery, or by the bones of Thorth, I'll split your head, and go on without a guide. Vernia of Reabon will take her own life rather than submit to the dictates of this reptilian rogo. As it is, we may be too late."

The pirate scrambled hastily to his feet.

"I'll guide you, Majesty, and quickly," he promised, "but we must circle the Valkar village to reach the compound. Otherwise we should not be permitted to go far."

He set off at once through the tall, rustling grass, with Grandon, scarbo in hand, just behind him, and Kantar bringing up the rear. After a short walk Grandon heard, only a little way ahead of them, the chatter of human conversation and the croaking of Valkars, punctuated by the sharp clanking of metal.

So Lan turned. "The compound is just ahead," he whispered. "Those are the sounds made by the metal workers and their overseers."

The three crept cautiously forward now. So Lan, parting the grass, pointed to an enclosure by a paling of metal bars, in the center of which was a large, moss-covered mound.

Grandon's heart gave a great bound as he saw Vernia standing beside a pile of knives. Then he cried out in anguish, and would have leaped forward had not Kantar detained him, as he saw her snatch the knife and attempt to plunge it into her bosom. But it was instantly shaken from her grasp by one of the yellow slaves who had grasped her wrist. Fortunately, Grandon's involuntary cry had not been heard over that bedlam of sound, and so the three men still crouched there, undetected.

"What are we to do now, Majesty?" asked Kantar.

"I don't know, Gunner. Let me think—let me plan. A sudden rush and a shower of tork bullets might be best. And yet, it might mean the death of Vernia. We must try to think of a better scheme."

He turned to the yellow man who still crouched in the grass beside him. "You may go now, So Lan. You have earned your freedom."

"Your Majesty has saved the life of So Lan," replied the pirate, "and he is not ungrateful. Permit him to remain near you, that he may be of assistance in the rescue of Her Majesty, your wife."

"How? You are unarmed. But wait. Perhaps we can use you, for you could pass unnoticed among the slaves where one of us would be instantly detected."

"I but await Your Majesty's commands," replied So Lan, bowing low.

C H A P T E R VII

HUMAN SACRIFICE

VERNIA STROVE TO WRENCH HER ARM
free, but she was helpless in the grip of the filthy and ragged
Hui Sen. He grinned the hideous, toothless grin of the Huitsenni, and pushed a fresh quid of kerra spores into his cheek
as he dragged her toward the gate.

"Where are you taking me?" she demanded.

"First to the burrow of His Majesty, Grunk, Rogo of the
Valkars, that he may give you his commands in person. Then,
if he does not change his mind, which he sometimes does, but
which I hope will not be the case in this instance, I will take
you to my own burrow."

"Suppose that I should offer you the wealth and position of
a prince—make you rich and powerful beyond your fondest

dreams. Would you help me to escape?"

"That would be impossible, Majesty. I am not so strong a swimmer that I could reach your country from here, and the Valkars would not give us time to build a boat."

"But there is a small sailboat, provisioned and ready, in the harbor where your boats stop for fresh water. If we could reach it and get away by night, surely you are enough of a navigator to sail it to Reabon. And what I promise, I will perform."

"We will speak of this later, Majesty," replied Hui Sen. "Just now I must take you before the Rogo." He entered into a short, croaking conversation with the Valkar guard at the gate, who then swung it open, permitting them to pass.

As they threaded their way between the moss-covered mounds toward the burrow of Grunk, Hui Sen looked cautiously about him as if fearful of being overheard, then said: "I cannot deny, Majesty, that the station and wealth of a prince would be a great temptation to me, for I have lived in squalor these many years. And while living thus, my only solace has been in dreams of splendor and power. But the risk would be tremendous. To pass the Valkar guards would not be easy. To cross the swamp without a Valkar guide would be next to impossible. Were it not for that swamp, my people would long ago have exterminated the Valkars. There is also the possibility that the boat might not be there, in which event the Valkars would be sure to find us, and I, at least, would be horribly punished. Added to these, and by far not the least of the considerations, would be the fact that I should lose you as my mate."

"On that score, at least, you may set yourself at rest," said Vernia. "Does the hahoe take the mate of the marmelot, or the awoo the mate of the ramph? Grandon of Terra is my mate, and sooner or later he will find this island, wipe the Valkars from the face of the planet, and all with them who have offered me indignity."

"Grandon of Terra will not find this place," said Hui Sen, confidently. "You cannot frighten me with his name, mighty as I know it to be."

"You will remember, also," continued Vernia, "that the mate of the marmelot is not without claws. I promise you that, if you offer me any indignity, I will slay you at the first opportunity, and myself, also. Sleeping or waking, your life will never be safe, if you drag me off to your stinking burrow."

"That I know you would do," replied Hui Sen, seemingly impressed, "for the women of Reabon were ever jealous of their honor. Night and day, I would always be on my guard, unless, perchance, you should learn to love me."

"Love you? Why, you greasy yellow beast! You unspeakable filth! Sooner would I love a warty Valkar." This was said with flashing eyes, and an imperious mien that humbled the yellow man.

"I mean no offense, Majesty," he whined. "Even a worm may look at a star with the hope that, inaccessible as it seems, it shines favorably upon him. But here we are at the burrow of the Rogo."

They were about to enter when Hui Sen halted and cocked his head to one side at the sound of a distant ululation, long drawn out, and exceedingly mournful.

"What was that?" asked Vernia.

"The cry of the guards," replied Hui Sen. "Sistabez, the great serpent, has come out of his cave."

The howling grew in volume as thousands of Valkar throats all over the village took it up. At this instant, Grunk, Rogo of the Valkars, emerged from his burrow, accompanied by Lui Sen and his two immense Valkar guards, both of which, with their noses elevated and their mouths open from ear to ear, were howling lustily. The din had now grown so loud that speech was impossible, but Grunk, after staring fixedly at Vernia and Hui Sen for a moment with his great, gold-rimmed

eyes, made a sign that they should follow him, and strode off
between the moss-covered mounds toward the place from
which the howling had first come. Judging from the mob
of Valkars, male and female, old and young, which was heading in the same direction, it was evident that the entire village
had turned out.

The hurrying, jostling crowd respectfully made way for the
Rogo and his party, and they soon reached the edge of the
village. Here a narrow path led up a rugged hillside, strewn
with boulders and sparsely dotted with low-growing shrubs.
At intervals of about a hundred feet along this path, heavy
iron stakes had been driven into the ground.

To the farthest of these stakes, a luckless yellow slave had
already been fastened. Another was being secured to the
next stake, and two guards were marching a third up to the
next.

Suddenly every voice was hushed, and Vernia saw an enormous and hideous head round a curve in the rugged hillside.
It was about ten feet in length, and six in width at its broadest
point, tapering down to a square muzzle about two feet across.
This massive head was reared on a thick neck fully four feet
in diameter, to a height of about twenty feet above the ground.
Behind it trailed a tremendous length of sinuous body. In
color it was muddy green above, and the under scales were
a greenish lemon-yellow.

Languidly, unhurriedly, the monster glided down the path,
surveying the immense crowd of Valkars and yellow slaves
before it with apparent indifference. Presently, as it came to
the first slave that had been bound in its path, it paused, and
leisurely arched its neck. The other two slaves had, meanwhile, been tethered and left to their fate. All three unfortu-
nates struggled desperately, and cried out for mercy, but as the
serpent poised over the first wretch, he ceased his struggles
and importunites.

There was a quick, downward dart of that massive head, so

swift that the eye could scarcely follow, and a single shriek from the victim as the immense jaws closed upon him, breaking his bonds like cobwebs. Then a significant lump slid down the serpent's throat to disappear in its tremendous coils.

Leisurely the snake crawled forward once more, seized and swallowed its next shrieking victim. It paused for a moment, but as it moved on toward the third victim, a fourth was quickly chained in its path.

"Sistabez is hungry today," Hui Sen said to Vernia.

The snake swallowed the third victim, and continued on toward the fourth.

"He is very hungry," said Hui Sen.

As it moved forward this time, the serpent's red forked tongue darted from its mouth, appearing and disappearing with the rapidity of lightning.

"He grows angry," cried Hui Sen, in alarm.

At this instant, Grunk turned and croaked something to two guards, who came toward Vernia.

"What did he say?" she asked Hui Sen.

"He said," replied that worthy, "that Sistabez was angry because he had withheld the fair white prisoner from him. He ordered the guards to tie you to the fifth stake."

With a sudden wrench, Vernia freed her wrist from the grasp of the yellow man, than turned to flee. But before she had taken ten steps the Valkar guards had her. The fourth victim shrieked his last as she was dragged to the stake and securely bound. The two guards retreated precipitately as the serpent advanced, this time traveling more swiftly than before, its tongue flashing like red forked lightning.

THE WRATH OF THE SERPENT

CROUCHING IN THE GRASS NEAR THE slave compound with Kantar and So Lan, Grandon saw the yellow slave who had prevented Vernia from taking her own life, lead her through the gate.

"Where is he taking her?" he asked So Lan.

"They walk toward the burrow of Grunk," replied So Lan. "I think she will be taken before the Rogo of the Valkars."

"And then?"

"Grunk will probably decide which of the slaves is to take her to his burrow."

"I believe so, Majesty. No alarm has been sounded, so I take it that I have not yet been missed. The Valkar that was pursuing me was a hunter I had encountered at some distance from the village."

"Very well. Suppose you—but wait! What is that howling sound?"

"The guards are warning the Valkars that Sistabez, the great serpent, has awakened, and is emerging from his den. No need to go into the village now, for everyone will attend the sacrifice."

"Sistabez?"

"A huge snake worshipped by the Valkars as a god. When he comes forth, they chain slaves in his pathway, in order that he may not raid the village. Naturally they value their own lives above those of their prisoners."

"And Vernia is a prisoner! Can you get us quickly to this place of sacrifice?"

"We will have to circle the village, Majesty. It will take quite a while."

"Then hurry."

"This way." So Lan dashed off through the tall grass with Grandon and Kantar at his heels.

Before they had gone far, it was obvious to Grandon that the Valkars would reach the place of sacrifice long before they would. Fuming at the delay, he kept urging the little yellow man to his best paces, but though he was willing enough, his short legs would not carry him nearly so fast as the two impatient white men could travel.

The howling from the village was deafening for some time, but to Grandon's surprise, it suddenly ceased altogether.

"Sistabez has reached the place of sacrifice," panted So Lan. "The Valkars always quit their howling when he is ready to take his first victim."

Grandon, who could restrain his impatience no longer, now thrust his puffing and nearly exhausted guide out of the way, and dashed forward at top speed. He needed no guide a moment later, for the shriek of the snake's first victim rang in his ears. Closely followed by Kantar, he bounded straight toward that sound. A short time later he heard, much closer, the cry of the second victim, then, still closer, the third, and finally the fourth.

A moment later, he bounded out into the open space at the base of the hill, in front of which the Valkars had assembled. Vernia had just been bound to the stake, and the two Valkars who had tied her were fleeing for their lives as the great serpent advanced toward her.

"Try to keep the crowd back, Gunner," he shouted to Kantar as he whipped out his scarbo and sprinted for the stake. The two Valkars who had bound Vernia tried to stop him, but he elevated the muzzle of his tork, and sprayed them with needle-like bullets. One of them fell, gasping and kicking his last, for Grandon had loaded the weapon with a clip of projectiles he had found in the belt pouch of San Thoy, which contained enough poison to kill a dozen men. He dispatched the other toad man with his scarbo.

A few swift strides carried him to Vernia's side, and two strokes of his scarbo freed her. She was so overcome by the ordeal through which she had just passed that she swooned, and would have fallen, had not Grandon sheathed his scarbo and caught her up in his arms.

All this took place in less than a minute, and during this time the tork of the gunner had been popping to good purpose, as attested by the ring of fallen Valkars which had been bold enough to rush him. Now, as Grandon dashed back into the tall grass with Vernia in his arms, Kantar ran behind him to cover his retreat.

The serpent, meanwhile, had not shown any interest in these proceedings, but had crawled on past the stake to seize and swallow the two Valkars that still lay kicking on the ground.

"What kind of bullets are you using?" Grandon asked the gunner, as they plunged into the grass.

"Deadly," he replied.

"Put in a clip of solid bullets for a moment," directed Grandon, "and give the big snake a half dozen or so in the neck."

Kantar chuckled as he swiftly carried out the Earthman's instructions. "A good idea, Majesty," he said. "It will give the ugly toads something to do besides chasing us."

Kantar was the best marksman in the Reabonian army, either with a tork or mattork, and it was child's play for him to quickly place the bullets as he had been directed. The effect on the huge serpent was instantaneous. With its forked tongue playing so rapidly that the eye could scarcely follow, and an angry hissing sound that was almost like the roar of steam escaping from a locomotive, it coiled and struck again and again into the closely packed crowd of Valkars, a tremendous living engine of destruction. Before, it had only been satisfying its hunger. Now it was taking swift and horrible toll of those creatures which it believed responsible for its hurts.

With his own tork, Grandon, meanwhile, shot down a score of Valkars that had followed them, giving the gunner time to reload with the deadly projectiles. As they hurried forward once more, they were joined by So Lan, who had armed himself with a hook, mace, and knife taken from one of the fallen Valkars.

"Take care not to scratch yourself or anyone else with those weapons," warned Kantar, as they trotted through the grass. "We have no Valkar blood for an antidote, now."

"I have seen to that," replied So Lan. He raised the flap of his belt pouch, and disclosed a slice of still quivering flesh. "This will serve all of us if need arise."

It was evident that the Valkars were well occupied with their own troubles, as none appeared to molest them for some time. They soon found the path which led from the village to the swamp, and had followed this for about a mile, when Vernia, still in her husband's arms, recovered consciousness, and demanded to be set on her feet.

"I can carry you all the way to the boat, if need be," Grandon protested.

"No, Bob. You must save your strength, for we will have need of it. I can walk as well as any of you, now. Besides, your hands must be free to grasp your weapons. The Valkars may catch up with us at any time."

"I rather think they're pretty well occupied with their own troubles, right now. But try it for a while if you must. I can carry you again if you tire."

They set off at a fast walk, but had not gone far when Kantar, who was at the rear, softly called: "Majesty."

Grandon turned. "What is it?"

"Something following us. I see the grass waving."

"We'll make a stand," Grandon decided, "and give them a warm reception if they're Valkars."

A moment later, a short yellow man appeared in the pathway. He was followed by five more. Grandon recognized the leader as San Thoy, and whipping out his scarbo, advanced toward him, ignoring the others.

"So," he thundered, "you are the yellow filth who abducted my wife!"

San Thoy cringed, then dropped to his knees with right hand extended palm downward, as Grandon towered above him with upraised scarbo.

"No, no, Majesty! Spare me! There is a misunderstanding! I tried to rescue Her Majesty. We stopped at the cabin to wait for daylight, that I might take her to the Reabonian coast."

"Ah! Then you did not, with your unwelcome advances, drive her forth into the night to be captured by the Valkars?" turned to Kantar. "Lend this rakehell of Huitsen your blade, Gunner, that I may settle accounts with him."

San Thoy quaked with fear.

"But I am no swordsman, Majesty," he whined, "to oppose the mightiest blade on Zorovia. It would be murder. Besides, as Thorth is my witness, I do not recall offering any affront to her Gracious Majesty. My head became so addled with kova that I did not know I had been wounded and captured by the Valkars until this morning."

"I perceive," said Grandon, contemptuously, "that you are a liar and a coward as well as a rogue. What shall I do with the vermin, Gunner?"

"Strike off his head, sire, and leave his foul remains to the jungle scavengers."

"Right. It is the least that he deserves."

San Thoy cringed, expecting the death blow as Grandon raised his blade. But it did not fall, for at this moment Vernia caught his arm.

"Please, Bob, I can't let you do it," she said. "Spare him for my sake."

"It is for your sake that I would put an end to him," replied Grandon. "To permit him to live after—"

"Please. Remember Tholto, the marshman. You would have slain him for a similar offense, but spared him because I requested it. And he afterward saved my honor when I was in the power of Zanaloth of Mernerum. Later, he saved both our lives."

"True," replied Grandon, "But this vile creature is no more like Tholto than a Valkar is like me. Yet, because it is your request, I can not do otherwise than spare him." He spurned the groveling San Thoy with his foot. "Get up," he commanded, "and remember that you are indebted to the Torroga of Reabon for your worthless life."

"Then may we accompany Your Majesties through the swamp to the coast?" asked one of the escaped slaves who had come up with San Thoy. "We could not find the way, unaided, and we are not armed against the monsters we should be sure to encounter."

"We are not anxious for such company," replied Grandon, "but you may follow behind us."

They set off once more, Grandon leading, closely followed by Vernia, So Lan, and Kantar. At a respectful distance behind tramped San Thoy and his Band.

A short march took them to the treacherous swamp, where Grandon was able to make much better time than on his previous trip through it, by backtracking in his own footsteps. But their progress was slow at best, and it was not long before there came an imploring cry from San Thoy.

"The Valkars are coming! Give us aid! Save us!"

"They don't deserve it," said Grandon, "but after all, they are human beings, and unarmed and in danger. Bring your comrades forward, San Thoy," he called, "and you, Gunner, guard the rear. If you can't handle things, let me know, and I'll come back with you."

Kantar stood aside until San Thoy and his comrades had time to close in behind So Lan. Then he fell in behind the last man, and as they marched forward, glanced back from time to time to note the proximity of the enemy. He soon saw that the Valkars were gaining rapidly on them, and also that they were not keeping to the trail, but were spreading out in a crescent shaped line, evidently with the intention of surrounding them. After communicating this intelligence to Grandon, he began picking off with his tork such Valkars as came dangerously close.

Presently, when the dull-witted Valkars began to realize that to expose themselves to the gunner's deadly aim meant sure death, they took advantage of cover. This slowed them a bit, but still their pace was swifter than that of Grandon's party, as their webbed feet gave them considerable advantage in traveling over the swampy ground. Soon the two horns of their crescent caught up with Grandon, who began using his tork as frequently as Kantar, though with not quite such deadly precision. With sword or scarbo he had not met his equal on all Zorovia, but there was only one Kantar the Gunner, and

Grandon, though an excellent shot, bowed to his uncanny skill with the weapon.

Between the two of them, Grandon and Kantar managed to keep their enemies at bay until they reached the more solid footing of the sparsely wooded hills. But in the meantime, the horns of the crescent had closed in front of them. On the firmer ground, however, their speed exceeded that of the Valkars, and since they no longer feared those behind them, but only those in front and at the sides, he changed his formation, massing the non-combatants in the center, while he and the gunner ranged on each side.

Only a few of the Valkars had succeeded in getting ahead of them, and these succumbed to the marksmanship of the two men. Then Grandon ordered a swift charge across the hill that confronted them, and beyond which was the thick fern forest that fringed the bay. When he reached the brow of the hill, he glanced back and saw that several hundred Valkars had already emerged from the swamp, while at least a thousand swarmed through the muck and water behind them. But the sight of this vast force did not dismay him, for he knew that his party could easily outrun them on the firm ground that lay ahead, and that they would have ample time to launch the little boat which San Thoy had moored near the cabin.

They dashed down the rugged hillside, and plunged into the fern forest, just as the front lines of their pursuers swept over the brow of the hill. But Grandon had scarcely taken fifty steps into the forest shadows, when a heavy body fell on his back from the branches above, knocking him to the ground. It was quickly followed by a half dozen more, and though the Earth-man managed to struggle to his feet, his arms were pinioned behind him, and his weapons taken away. He had led his party directly into an ambush of yellow pirates. Kantar, he observed, had been served in like manner.

Suddenly then, as if by magic, a whole army of Huitsenni appeared, stepping from behind tree trunks, bushes, and rocks, and dropping from the dense tangle of branches overhead. The little party was completely surrounded and hopelessly outnumbered.

Waddling toward them through the ranks of the pirates, who respectfully made way for him, Grandon now recognized Thid Yet, Romojak of the Navies of Huitsen.

Thid Yet expectorated a red stream of kerra juice, and grinned toothlessly, as he bowed before Grandon and Vernia.

"I am gratified that we arrived in time to save Your Majesties from the Valkars," he said. "Guest chambers have been prepared for you and your warrior aboard my flagship." His eyes next fell on the cowering San Thoy. "So, traitor, we meet again. I doubt not that His Majesty of Huitsen will contrive exquisite tortures for you when he has heard the story of your perfidy. Seize him, men." His glance next fell on So Lan and the other unarmed yellow men who formed the balance of the party. "Who are you?" he asked.

"We are from various crews, Excellency, sent ashore for water, and captured in engagements with the Valkars, who held us as slaves," replied So Lan.

"So? Then report to my mojo who will assign you to new berths."

At this moment, one of Thid Yet's aids ran up to announce that the Valkars were attacking in force.

"Tell the mattork crews to make a stand at the edge of the woods and mow them down without mercy," commanded Thid Yet. "These warty monsters need a lesson, and now is the time to read them one they will not soon forget."

As they marched toward the harbor, Grandon heard the rattle of mattork fire, which continued for several minutes. Then it suddenly stopped, and he concluded that the Valkars, seeing that they had run into an ambush, had retreated. This he afterward learned was really the case.

They found the beach lined with the small boats of the Huitsenni, while the pirate fleet rode at anchor less than a quarter of a mile from the entrance to the cove. Grandon, Vernia, Kantar, and San Thoy were rowed to the flagship in the boat of Thid Yet. Back on the deck of the vessel once more, the Romojak gave swift orders.

"Return Her Majesty of Reabon to her former quarters, and keep her door constantly guarded," he told his mojo. "His Majesty, here, together with his warrior and our treacherous mojak, will have to be put in irons, and confined below decks. And keep two armed guards constantly before their door. They escaped too easily the last time."

Vernia was led away to her cabin, and the three men were fitted with thick metal collars, to which heavy chains were attached, linking them together. Then they were lowered down a hatchway, and marched along a corridor, to be thrust into a small and exceedingly filthy room. The door of heavy serali planks was barred, and Grandon heard two guards take their places before it.

Soon the anchors were hoisted and the sails unfurled. With the flagship in the lead, the fleet once more sailed southward.

C H A P T E R IX

THE SECRET GATE

THE ROOM IN WHICH GRANDON, KANTAR, and San Thoy had been confined on the pirate ship was immediately below the deck, hence free from the bilge water which swished in the hold below, though not far from the offensive odor which arose from it. Light filtered down to them through the loosely fitted deck planking, and also shone through several small holes, each about two inches in diameter, which were bored high up in the ship's side, evidently to serve as loopholes through which torks might be fired. But they also acted, to some extent, as ventilators, making it possible for the prisoners to breathe the fresh sea air by pressing their noses to them, and admitting enough light to partly dispel the cheerless gloom of the humid and stuffy interior.

The chains with which the three men were fastened together by their metal collars, were about five feet in length, the gunner being in the middle, and Grandon and San Thoy at either end. After they had sniffed the fresh air for some time, the three sat down, as if by mutual consent, resting their backs against the rough wall.

"Well, Gunner, it looks as if Thid Yet has us in a tight place this time," said Grandon.

"We have been in tighter, Majesty," replied Kantar.

"True. But this arrangement presents a rather knotty problem. In the first place, there are two guards outside the door now instead of one. In the second place, the wily Romojak has chained us to that carrion," indicating San Thoy, "who will surely make an outcry if we attempt an escape. Of course we can throttle him, or dash his brains out against the wall, but it would be difficult to slay him so quietly that the guards outside the door would not hear, and at least suspect something amiss."

San Thoy shifted his quid of kerra spores and spat through a crack.

"May I remind Your Majesty," he said, "that I am as anxious to escape from Thid Yet as you? I am to be slain by slow torture upon my arrival in Huitsen."

"True," replied Grandon. "Perhaps you will be worthy of our confidence on that score, if on no other."

At this moment one of the guards opened the door to admit a menial from the galley. This greasy and profusely perspiring individual carried a tray on which were three large eating bowls and three smaller drinking bowls. These he set before the prisoners, and hastily withdrew, as if fearful that they might attack him.

When the door had closed behind him, San Thoy quickly rolled up his red quid and stuck it to the back of his left hand. Then with his right he dipped into his eating bowl, feeding greedily and from time to time taking copious drafts from his drinking bowl to wash down the food which he could only mumble.

Grandon examined the mixture in the bowl before him. It smelled savory enough, and upon tasting it, he found that it was a mixture of flaked fish and chopped mushrooms, stewed together in a sauce that was highly spiced and quite peppery. His drinking bowl contained freshly brewed kova, slightly weak, but palatable.

"Not bad for prison fare," he commented to the gunner, who he noticed had begun to make good progress with his meal.

"It's the one good thing about these yellow vermin which I am willing to concede. They can certainly cook," replied Kantar.

"We are fortunate in being imprisoned with royalty," said San Thoy, smacking his lips. "We should not otherwise be so well fed." His meal over, he deftly flipped the red quid from the back of his left hand into his toothless mouth, and resumed his mumbling.

For many days the three men were kept in their stuffy prison. They were fed three times a day, but otherwise saw nothing of their captors. By peering through the loopholes they could amuse themselves in the daytime by watching such birds, fish, and reptiles as came within their line of vision.

During this period, however, they had not been idle in attempting to find some way of escape. It was the gunner whose ingenuity devised the means for the first step in this direction. Although he had been disarmed, he had not been deprived of his small packet of tools, commonly carried by every man of his profession, which were for the purpose of taking apart and assembling mattorks that some times jammed or failed in other ways to work properly and smoothly. These tools, like those used by terrestial watchmakers, were small and fine, as the mechanisms on which they were used were extremely delicate.

He began on the lock which held Grandon's metal collar around his neck. The task seemed hopeless at first, for the Huitsenni were skilled in the fabrication of such things as fetters, weapons, and instruments of torture. But after many days of patient work, he eventually had the satisfaction of springing the clasp, making it possible for the Earth-man to remove his collar by simply bending it back on the hinge. Grandon then worked on the gunner's collar under his direction, and not being mechanically inclined, took considerable time in achieving the same favor for his henchman.

This done, Grandon suggested that the gunner open the lock on San Thoy's collar. The task did not please him, but he was too well trained a soldier to quarrel with the orders of his sovereign, and so carried out his distasteful duty without a murmur.

They had got this far with their plans for escape, and were considering what their next move should be, when Kantar, who had been standing with his eye to a loophole, suddenly informed the Earth-man that he saw land.

Grandon leaped to a hole beside him, and peered out. He saw that the ship was entering what appeared to be the narrow channel of a fiord. The rugged cliffs, sparsely clad in places with stunted conifers, towered to a tremendous height above the placid water, which calmly reflected their beetling frowns. Sharp commands and the creaking of pulleys were heard above them as the sails were lowered. Then oars rattled, and splashed into the water, thrust through the rowing holes beneath them.

San Thoy had told Grandon and Kantar that Huitsen, the capital city of the Huitsenni, could be reached from the sea only by way of a hidden passage through towering cliffs. If he had spoken truth, then this was the beginning of that passageway, and the time left to them for freeing themselves and Vernia, and attempting to escape, was short indeed. The pirate himself confirmed this a moment later, as he too sprang up to peer through a loophole.

"This is the way to the secret gate," he said. "Watch, and you will see how it is opened."

Grandon's first thought was that they must immediately attempt escape, for once in the notorious port of peril, this would undoubtedly prove impossible. Yet a rash attempt now seemed equally hopeless. He had counted on darkness as an ally, but it was yet midafternoon, and the probability was that the fleet would dock ere the black, moonless night of Venus should descend. He had expected to strike that very evening, when the cook's helper would bring them their repast. Leaving San Thoy to deal with the helper, he and the gunner had planned to spring upon the two guards who stood outside the door. Could the deed have been accomplished without great noise, the rest would not have been impracticable; for under cover of darkness it would have been possible to rescue Vernia from her cabin, steal a boat, and be off.

But now, it seemed, they must make new plans.

"How soon will we dock, San Thoy?" he asked.

"In a very short time now, Majesty," was the reply.

"Before dark?"

"Oh, long before."

Grandon pondered for a moment. Then he spoke to Kantar. "We'll have to think up a new scheme, Gunner. And when the time comes, we'll have to think fast."

"I will look for a sign from you when the time does come," replied Kantar.

"And I, also, Majesty," echoed San Thoy. Then he exclaimed: "See! They are opening the secret entrance!"

The channel had narrowed now, so much that it seemed the ship's oars would be shattered against the jagged cliffs. And straight ahead was what appeared to be a solid wall of rock, barring their further progress. Astounded, Grandon saw that a crooked crack extending medially from top to bottom was slowly widening as the two halves of the wall ahead, each

of which must have weighed thousands of tons, moved apart
and slid into the cliffs on each side.

The ship nosed through the opening and into a dark cavern.
The lights flashed on, and revealed a stalactite-festooned ceiling over head, while the peaks of white stalagmites, projecting above the surface of the water, made it obvious that the
floor of the cave had not always been flooded. Save for the
gong which timed the strokes of the rowers, and the splashing
of the oars, the place was as quiet as a tomb, its placid waters
gleaming mirror-like ahead of the ship, and rippling in the
spreading wake like molten jet shot with silver reflections.

Presently daylight appeared ahead, and the ship's lights
were turned off. A moment later they emerged through a
high, arched opening into a canal. The straight banks were lined
with masonry, evidently to prevent the salt water from seeping
through and spoiling the crops of edible mushrooms, food
ferns, and kerra ferns which were cultivated in orderly fields
on either side. Those who worked in these fields, San Thoy
said, were slaves who represented most of the races and nation-
alities of Zorovia, some captured in coastal raids, but most
taken from ships that had fallen prey to the yellow pirates.

Swiftly propelled by the lusty strokes of the rowers, and
again aided by the bat-wing sails, which had been unfolded
as soon as the cave mouth was left behind, the ship glided into
a circular land-locked harbor, lined with docks built of serali
wood and set on pilings of the same tough material. Behind
the docks were warehouses of white stone, and beyond these,
at the far side, Grandon could see the conical roofs and upper
structures of what appeared to be a large and populous city,
principally composed of odd, hive-shaped buildings unlike anything he had ever seen or heard of, either on Earth or Venus.

Thousands of queer, bat-winged craft of the pirates were
moored at the docks, and many more rode at anchor in the
harbor. There were also a large number of merchant and
fishing ships captured by the Huitsenni, and brought in as

prizes. Some of these were undergoing alterations, being fitted with the bat-wing sails, and otherwise converted for the use of the yellow men.

Still peering through his loophole, Grandon saw that the flagship was nearing the dock. Soon the long oars beneath him were drawn in, and ropes were cast to waiting Huitsenni, who made them fast.

From almost directly above Grandon's head, a gangplank was lowered striking the dock with a heavy thud. Down the plank walked Thid Yet, Romojak of the Navies of Huitsen, escorting Vernia. The princess looked deathly pale, but showed no other sign of fear. With her head held proudly erect, and graceful carriage, she showed only disdain for her squat, greasy captor, slouching along beside her. Behind them strode a guard of six pirates, drawn scarbos in their hands.

A great lumbering one-wheeled vehicle, its cab supported on an inner idling-wheel at its center, rumbled up to the dock. These vehicles were common everywhere on Zorovia, but the beasts that drew this one were not. Hitched, one before and one behind the great wheel, they were larger than Norman Horses, covered with long white curly hair of silky texture, and each armed with three twisted horns, one curving forward from the tip of the nose, and the other two arching above the eyes. Their ankles, also were armed with sharp bony spurs, projecting toward the front on the forelegs, and toward the back on the hind legs. Their hoofs were split into three sections, each of which was armed with a claw.

Thid Yet assisted Vernia to enter the vehicle, then clambered up after. The drivers shouted to their beasts, and the huge wheel lumbered away.

"Where are they taking her?" Grandon asked San Thoy.

"To the palace, no doubt," the yellow man replied, "where we, too, will be taken shortly."

"If my plan works, I'll go to the palace, but not as a prisoner," Grandon told his two companions. "We will attain at least temporary liberty if you throw off your collars when I raise my right hand, then follow me."

Grandon saw the loot from his camp, and the weapons and accouterments of his Fighting Traveks, carried ashore. Then the door of their prison was flung open, and a self-important mojo, accompanied by four guards, all carrying their scarbos in their hands, ordered them out.

They were ushered up a companionway, and on reaching the deck, were forced into a line of yellow men who, laden with their loot, were hurrying ashore.

They had reached the center of the swaying gangplank when Grandon suddenly raised his right hand. Simultaneously, the three prisoners threw off the collars which their captors had, up until then, believed to be locked. Before they could act, the Earth-man had turned and dived into the water beneath, swiftly followed by his two companions.

THE PORT OF PERIL

CONFINED IN THE IDENTICAL CABIN from which she had shortly before been stolen by San Thoy, Vernia hoped against hope that Grandon would find some way to rescue her. But as the pirates sailed southward, day after day, and no word of any kind came from him hope began to fade.

Day and night, two armed guards were kept constantly before her door, the only exit from her cabin. At first she attempted to question them, but they would not answer. Then she tried quizzing the slave who brought her meals. He was ready enough to converse about her desires in the way of food, but when she tried interrogating him about Grandon or about their destination, he always professed ignorance.

Thus was her mind burdened with double anxiety—the fear that Grandon might be tortured or slain, and the certainty that each day was bringing her nearer to the lascivious monster who had bribed the Huitsenni to capture her. Although no mention of his name had passed the lips of any of the pirates in her presence, she was positive that the instigator of the plot was none other than the pleasure-bloated tyrant, Zanaloth, Torrogo of Mernerum—Zanaloth, at the mere mention of whose name comely maidens would shudder, whose scarlet suite was notorious throughout all Zorovia, and whose subjects with sweethearts, sisters, daughters, or wives of more than ordinary beauty lived in constant dread that their loved ones might be summoned to the seraglio of the tyrant.

Her days she spent in gazing out through the small window of her cabin, her nights in restless turning and tossing upon her sleeping shelf. But a day came when the shutter of her window was closed so that she could not see out. Her cabin door, also, was locked. Evidently, she thought, something was about to take place on or near the ship which the Huitsenni did not wish her to see. A short time later she heard the noises of the bat-wing sails being lowered and the oars shipped.

For some time she heard only the sound of commands and the splashing of oars. Presently the oars were unshipped, and there was the grating shock of the vessel grinding its side against some solid object. Then came the tramp of many feet on the deck.

Shortly thereafter, her door was unlocked and flung open. Thid Yet stood before her. "Come," he said. "We have arrived in Huitsen."

In Huitsen! Then the reason for the closed shutter and locked door was apparent. They had not let her see the concealed entrance to this hidden lair of the yellow pirates because she would not be expected to remain here permanently— because she was to be sold into slavery outside the domains of the Huitsenni.

She stepped out of the cabin. There was nothing else for her to do. Thid Yet led her toward the gangplank, and a guard of six pirates fell in behind them. She glanced around, hoping to catch sight of Grandon or Kantar. Concealing, as best she could, her disappointment at not seeing them, she walked across the plank with her captor.

The one-wheeled cart was no novelty to Vernia. She had seen many like it in her own country. But the fearsome, three-horned white beasts that were hitched to it were creatures she had never seen or heard of before.

"Zandars," said Thid Yet, noting her look of surprise. "They make strong beasts of burden and admirable chargers for our warriors to ride. We get them from the White Ibbits who inhabit the Mountains of Eternal Snow, far to the south. Let me help you."

The Romojak climbed in with her, and the heavy vehicle trundled away. The six guards trotted beside it, three on a side.

Traversing a narrow passageway between two stone warehouses, they emerged on a broad thoroughfare of heavy serali planking like that of which the dock was constructed. The hoofs of the zandars echoed hollowly as from a bridge, and the large single wheel of the cart made a sound much like the continuous rolling of thunder. This thoroughfare, like those which crossed it at various intervals, was lined with tall, hive-shaped buildings with oval windows and doorways. Like the warehouses, these buildings were of stone.

Yellow children, all of them naked and bald-headed scampered from in front of the vehicle and then paused to stare at them with their queer, cat-like eyes. Bald housewives, unclad save for short leathern aprons which depended from their ample waists, paused in their work to gaze at them through oval windows or from the doorsteps of their conical houses. Beside each doorstep, Vernia noticed that a hole had been cut in the planking, and many of the women held lines which hung down into these holes. She could not imagine what they were doing until one female suddenly jerked up a flopping, silvery scaled fish. She judged from this and the hollow sound of the planking that this section of the city was built over the inland sea.

There were few men about at this time of day, but those lolled against the houses or squatted on the doorsteps, squinting apathetically up at the passing vehicle. The entire hairless, toothless population, male and female, from the tiniest child playing naked in the street to the oldest crone fishing beside her doorstep, mumbled kerra spores and expectorated enormous quantities of the red juice.

The vehicle rapidly drew near to a towering structure which would have made a hundred of any of the lesser buildings around it. Like them, however, it was hive-shaped, and built of stone.

They rumbled through an immense oval doorway and halted. Thid Yet clambered down, and assisted Vernia to alight. They were in an enclosed court onto which several oval doors opened. Each doorway was guarded by two soldiers.

"This is the palace of Yin Yin, Rogo of Huitsen," said Thid Yet. "He has commanded that you be brought into his presence before we take you to our rendezvous with Zan—" He checked himself abruptly, and a look of vexation crossed his greasy features, as if he had unthinkingly mentioned some forbidden thing.

"Whether you finish the name or leave it unspoken does not matter," said Vernia. "I have known all along that the man who offered your Rogo such a fabulous sum for me that he dared the wrath of the mighty fighter who is my husband, and the power of unbeaten Reabon, to abduct me, could be none other than Zanaloth of Mernerum."

"After all, what does it matter, Zanaloth or another? You will know soon enough in any event. But come. His Majesty is expecting you, and may grow impatient."

Thid Yet conducted her through the nearest doorway, the six pirates falling in behind them, and the two guards saluting the Romojak as they entered. It led onto a gently sloping ramp which spiraled upward. The ramp was paved with black stone dotted with golden studs, which prevented the sandals of climbers from slipping as they ascended. At intervals of about fifty feet on either side were set ornate golden vessels, half filled with sand. Even had Thid Yet not utilized these freely on their way up, Vernia would have recognized their purpose by the fact that the sand was stained with spots of kerra juice.

After a considerable climb they came to a level passageway which led them to a large oval doorway hung with scarlet curtains and guarded by two yellow warriors. The guards saluted smartly at sight of the Romojak with his prisoner, and drew back the scarlet hangings.

Vernia was ushered into a circular room about two hundred feet in diameter, and so tremendously high that it had the appearance of a shaft, rather than a room. Its walls were of iridescent crystal blocks which reflected in many lovely hues the light that entered through four immense oval windows set in the top of the conical dome. At intervals of about fifteen feet it was circled by narrow balconies, the grille work of which was plated with gold and powdered with sparkling jewels. Behind the balconies many oval doorways led to apartments on the various levels. On these balconies were seated several hundred women and children, evidently members of the royal household. The floor was a single immense mirror which reflected every detail so clearly and faithfully that when Vernia looked down, it seemed that she was standing over a shaft of a depth equal to the height of the one which towered above her.

Vernia was led to the center of this magnificent hall where a circular divan, cut from a single block of clear crystal, supported a scarlet cushion at a height of about four feet above the floor. Squatting, cross-legged, in the middle of this cushion was an extremely corpulent yellow man, who, except for the scarlet cincture about his loins, was clad entirely in jewelry. Jewels blazed from the rings which all but concealed his pudgy fingers and toes, and flashed from his golden anklets, bracelets, armlets, and necklaces. Two immense diamonds stretched the lobes of his ears almost to his shoulders, and a large ruby sparkled on each of his broad nostrils. His bald head was the only unadorned part of his anatomy, but shone as brightly as if it, too, had been burnished by the royal lapidary.

Behind the throne stood two muscular guards, each leaning on a huge, two handed scarbo that reached from the floor to his chin. And back of these in a semi-circle were ranged purple-clad nobles and courtiers, beside each of which stood a jar of sand. At each side of the throne stood six slave-girls. Two held golden, jewel-encrusted cuspidors which the one at the right or the left extended, depending on which way the monarch turned his head when he wished to expectorate. Other girls bore the trays of newly opened kerra pods, ready for chewing, and still others, jeweled cups and pots of kova which were kept hot by small aromatic oil-burning lamps burning beneath them. And a young girl, scarcely more than half-grown, held a bundle of scarlet napkins, with one of which she wiped the royal chins from time to time—there were four of them—then passed the soiled cloths to an attendant.

As Thid Yet came before the throne with his beautiful prisoner, he bowed low with right hand extended palm downward, the universal Zorovian salute to royalty. Then he humbly waited for the ruler to speak.

Vernia, however, remained proudly erect, returning the appraising look of the creature on the throne with one of withering disdain.

Yin Yin, Rogo of Huitsen, spat into the jeweled cuspidor tendered by the girl at his right, submitted to having his multiple chins wiped, and then turned his cat-like eyes on his Romojak.

"Are you positive that this slender beauty, just budded into womanhood, is the Torroga of Reabon?" he asked.

"I am positive, Majesty," the Romojak replied. "She answers every description, and wears the scarlet and insignia of her imperial house."

Yin Yin turned to a purple-clad noble who stood near at hand.

"Fetch the painting," he commanded.

The man sped away, and vanished through one of the numerous doorways to return a moment later followed by two slaves who bore a life size portrait of Vernia. She instantly recognized it as having been taken from one of her war vessels, all of which carried such paintings before which every sailor and officers bowed each morning in token of his loyalty and submission to his imperial ruler.

Yin Yin ordered the painting set up a little to one side, then gazed alternately at the portrait and the living original who stood before him, for some time.

Presently he said: "It is indeed Vernia of Reabon, for she is, if anything, more beautiful than her picture. You have done well, Thid Yet. For this we reward you with a thousand kantols of land and a thousand keds of gold. We are just."

"Yin Yin, Rogo of Huitsen, is the fountainhead of justice," intoned the courtiers.

"May it please Your Majesty, I also captured her husband, the mighty fighter known as 'Grandon of Terra'," said Thid Yet, proudly.

"So I have heard," replied the monarch. "For this deed we reward you with a hundred strong slaves to work your land. We are just."

"Yin Yin, Rogo of Huitsen, is the living source of justice," chorused the courtiers.

"I have heard, also," continued Yin Yin, "that Grandon of Terra has escaped."

Thid Yet looked dumfounded, but at this news Vernia's
heart gave a great leap of joy.

"He escaped," the Rogo went on, "before he reached the
dock. Hence you, and you alone, are responsible. For this
carelessness we commend you to the expert offices of our headsman." One of the guards behind the throne here shouldered
his great, two handed scarbo, and stepped forward, but the
Rogo held up his hand. "Wait, Ez Bin," he commanded.
"Be not so impetuous." He turned again to Thid Yet. "If
you bring me not Grandon of Terra before ten days have
passed, then submit your neck to Ez Bin. We are just, but
we are merciful."

"Both just and merciful is Yin Yin, Rogo of Huitsen," cried
the courtiers.

The monarch moved a finger. Ez Bin returned to his post.
He moved another finger. Two of the six guards who had
followed Thid Yet and Vernia stepped up beside the Romojak.
Then the three bowed low before the throne with right hands
extended palms downward, and wheeling, left the room.

Yin Yin, meanwhile, refreshed himself with a cup of steaming kova, and stuffed his mouth with fresh kerra spores. He
mumbled them for some time in silence, ogling Vernia the
while, then spat, and said: "We do not wonder that a certain
torrogo, who shall be nameless, offered us the price of an empire for you. You are more than worth it."

"I care not for your compliments, you yellow filth," retorted Vernia, spiritedly.

"Nor we for your insults, my little beauty," replied Yin Yin.
"You are now but a chattel, a rather spirited chattel to be sure,
a regular she-marmelot of a chattel, but we like you that way.
We have subdued many such."

"To your everlasting dishonor, and their endless shame."

Yin Yin grinned. "That is a point on which you will find
many who will disagree with you. We will not argue it. We
never argue, for argument with us is always futile. It would

be unfair for us to argue." He turned to the noble who had brought him the picture. "Let us see our contract with—with this nameless torrogo," he commanded.

"Name Zanaloth of Mernerum, or keep him nameless. It is all one to me," said Vernia.

"Who told you that?" he asked, sharply.

"You could never guess, and I shall never tell you," replied Vernia, defiantly.

"Ah well. It doesn't matter. You will know soon enough." He took a scroll which the noble extended to him, and perused it for some time. "Hum. It is as I thought. This contract says we shall meet him before the harbor of the Island of the Valkars, one ship of his and one of ours, on the morning of the fourteenth day of the ninth endir in the four thousand and tenth year of Thorth. He will have, on the day previous, landed the slaves and treasure on the island, where the fear of the Valkars will prevent the former attempting to escape beyond the lines of the few guards who will be left to defend them.

"When our commander has satisfied himself that the slaves and treasure agreed upon have been left on the island, he will deliver to the Torrogo of Mernerum, or his agent, the person of Her Imperial Majesty, Vernia of Reabon.

"It does not say 'unharmed', nor is there anything in this contract to prevent our taking this Vernia of Reabon to be our handmaiden until such time as it may be necessary for her to sail for the rendezvous with Zanaloth."

He moved a finger, and two of the four guards who stood behind Vernia stepped up beside her.

"Take her to the seraglio," he commanded, "and tell Ufa to prepare her this night for the royal visit; for it may be that we will honor her with the light of our presence. We are generous."

"His Majesty, Yin Yin, Rogo of Huitsen, is most generous," chorused the courtiers, as Vernia her heart sinking within her, was led away.

C H A P T E R XI

THE SEA RATS

AS SOON AS GRANDON'S HANDS STRUCK
water, after he had dived from the gangplank, he turned them
so that his momentum carried him underneath the dock. A
moment later, his head bobbed to the surface, and he had the
satisfaction of seeing that Kantar and San Thoy had followed
his example, as both came up quite near him. From above
came the rattle of tork fire, the bullets cutting into the water
where the three fugitives had disappeared.

"You know this place," Grandon said to the yellow man.
"Where can we hide?"

"First we must get behind the warehouse," replied San Thoy.
"Follow me."

He struck out, and despite his portliness, proved to be an excellent swimmer. Grandon later learned that this was a racial and not an individual characteristic, as all Huitsenni, being reared on the water, swam fully as well as they walked, if not a shade better. Just now, however, he was sorely put to it to keep pace with the rotund pirate, while Kantar, the slowest of the three, trailed behind them.

San Thoy swiftly led them through a dark and narrow passage between two stone walls—the foundations of two warehouses. Above him, Grandon could hear shouts, curses, commands, and men running on the planking.

Once through the passage, the pirate waited for the others to come up with him. Here it was so murky that Grandon could barely see the faces of his companions.

"They will send boats and fast swimmers," whispered San Thoy, "but if we are quiet, it may be that we can elude them. It will soon be dark, and the darkness will be our ally. Follow closely behind me, and do not splash or talk."

Once more they set off, with the pirate in the lead. They were in a wilderness of posts, the piling that supported the planking of the street level, which was about fifteen feet above their heads. The rows of piles were broken at intervals of about fifty feet by the circular foundations of houses. Many of the fishing holes in front of these dwellings were open, admitting considerable daylight. And Grandon noticed that boats were moored in front of all of them, while deeply notched poles projecting down through the holes formed ladders by which they could be reached from above.

San Thoy, however, avoided the fronts of the houses with their fishing holes, and followed the lanes at the backs of the buildings, where it was so dark that objects were visible for only a few feet in any direction.

They had not gone far when it became obvious that a concerted pursuit had begun. Armed Huitsenni everywhere were swarming down the notched poles into the boats. Soon they were rowing about in all directions, flashing their lights, poking their oars into dark corners, and sending swimmers with knives gripped in their toothless gums, to explore the narrow places where the boats could not enter.

At first, it was not so difficult for San Thoy to avoid the searchers, but as they became more numerous his cunning was put more and more to the test. Time and again the three fugitives were compelled to hide behind pilings while boat-loads of searchers passed within a few feet of them. Although he had no opportunity to question him, Grandon judged that he was making for some definite hiding place, because, despite the many twists and turns to which he was forced by their pursuers, he continued to lead his companions always in the same general direction.

Presently, however, the three came to a place where it seemed that they would be able to advance no farther. Completely surrounded by the man hunters, and likely to be spied at any moment, they took refuge in the dark shadows of a cluster of piling. Lights flashed all about them, and when the beams came uncomfortably close, they submerged until they had passed.

One by one, however, the boats gradually drew off, until but one remained. It contained two pirates, naked save for leather breech clouts. One of them, having flashed his light among the piles, nudged his companion and said something that Grandon and the two with him were unable to hear. But his actions were eloquent of his meaning, for the next moment he and his fellow, with long knives gripped in their mouths, slid into the water, and silently swam toward the place of refuge occupied by the fugitives.

So quietly had the pirates entered the water, and so noiselessly were they approaching the clump of piling, that had it not been for their light, which shown from the prow of the boat, the fugitives would not have been aware of their coming. As it was, they were warned, but it seemed that there was little they could do, as not one of them was armed. To stand and fight seemed foolhardy, and to attempt to escape, worse than useless, for by shouting, the two man-hunters could quickly draw hundreds of their companions to cut off their escape.

In this dilemma, Grandon, as was his wont, thought swiftly and acted with celerity. As he saw it, there was but one way out, and if that failed they were doomed. Accordingly, he whispered rapid instructions to his two companions, and they took their places.

As the two pirates stealthily approached the clump of piles, they suddenly saw, directly in the path of the light from their boat, the face of San Thoy. He gave one frightened look at them, and turned, swimming rapidly in the opposite direction. With grunts of satisfaction, the two swimmers struck out after him, naturally taking the shortest and most direct route, which lay between two large posts about five feet apart. Their cat-like eyes gleamed with excitement of the chase. But just as they reached the space between the two large posts, two white arms shot out from behind them, and jerked the long knives from their mouths. Two keen blades flashed aloft, and swiftly descended. Two greasy corpses slipped from sight into the black depths.

Grandon and Kantar, treading water, thrust the blades into their belts as San Thoy returned, grinning broadly.

"Now," he said, "we can travel by boat."

The three fugitives quickly clambered aboard. The two six-pronged fishing spears lay along the gunwhale, and in back of the boat was a pile of nets.

Beneath these, Grandon and Kantar crept. San Thoy removed his insignia which proclaimed him a mojak of the Royal Navy, stripping himself down to his breech-clout. Then, looking much like one of the fishermen of Huitsen, he rowed away.

Grandon lay in the bottom of the boat beside Kantar, covered by nets which were eloquently redolent of recent contact with defunct fish, for what he judged to be about half an hour. Then San Thoy stopped, secured the boat to a pile, and lifting the nets, said: "Come. Follow me, and make no noise."

He let himself quietly into the water, and the two followed him. Grandon saw that they were not far from the rear of one of the conical houses, and that several other boats were moored nearby.

San Thoy led them to a point directly behind the house, and only a few feet from its circular stone walls. Then he said: "Grasp my belt, breathe deeply, and prepare to submerge."

With Grandon on one side and Kantar on the other, he then dived. Opening his eyes under water, Grandon saw a light glimmering some distance below them. They swam straight toward it. Soon they were in front of an oval door of thick glass framed with metal, and looking into a small chamber, beyond which was another similar door through which the light streamed. San Thoy seized a knocker which hung behind the door, and struck it three times. A face appeared, framed in the oval door beyond—the face of a yellow man. San Thoy signaled to him with one hand, whereupon he pulled a lever, and the door before them opened. Swiftly they were carried in by a sudden rush of water, and the door closed behind them. Now they were in a narrow chamber, completely filled with water. Grandon was growing air-hungry, desperately so, and he saw from Kantar's expression that he was in like case. But San Thoy did not appear in the least discommoded by holding his breath for so long.

The man behind the second door scrutinized the three for a moment, then exchanged several more signs with San Thoy, and pulled a second lever. At this, panels in the walls on both sides of them slid back, revealing a large screened opening, and the water receded so swiftly that both Grandon and Kantar, taken unawares, sprawled on the floor. They sprang to their feet, thankfully inhaling great lungfuls of the moist air. Then the inner door opened, and the man who stood beside it bade them enter.

They stepped inside, and as the guard closed the door after them, San Thoy addressed him.

"Greetings, warder and brother Chispok. Are the brothers in secret session?"

"They are in secret session, O mojak of the brotherhood," replied the yellow man.

Grandon was astounded to hear these two Huitsenni addressing each other as brother Chispoks; for he knew that a chispok was a large, scaly rodent inhabiting the sea shore or salt marshes, and spending a considerable share of its time in the water, literally a rat of the sea. It was a hideous creature, closely resembling its land cousin, the chipsa, and its name was formed from the two words, "chispa" and "pok", the latter word meaning "the sea". Thus were formed the names "Azpok", or "Sea of Az", and "Ropok", or "Sea of Ro". To be called a chispa or a chispok in Reabon, or almost any other civilized country of Zorovia, was a deadly insult. But here were two men saluting each other as brother Chispoks, without offense.

San Thoy continued his conversation with the guard.

"I have brought two recruits for our just and sacred cause, who came from the far land of Reabon," said San Thoy. "Your name, brother warder?"

"Fo San, brother mojak."

"And I am San Thoy. These are Grandon of Terra, Rogo of Uxpo and Torrogo of Reabon; and Kantar the Gunner, a citizen of Uxpo."

Fo San, apparently noting Grandon's sodden and bedraggled scarlet cincture for the first time, bowed low with right hand extended palm downward.

"The humble warder of the Chispoks salutes Your Majesty, the glory of whose deeds of valor has penetrated even to this remote corner of the world," he said.

Grandon returned the salute, and he and the gunner were invited to seat themselves.

"According to the rules of the order, you must await me here," said San Thoy. "I will go and speak to the romojak of the order. I am mojak of a lodge at the other end of the city. In the meantime, refreshments will be brought to you."

He walked to an oval metal door at the other end of the chamber, and gave three sharp raps. It swung open, and before it closed behind him, Grandon heard him exchange greetings with a yellow man on the other side.

A few minutes later, a boy came in, carrying a tray on which were bowls of steaming kova, grilled fish, and stewed mushrooms. Grandon and Kantar did full justice to the refreshments. While they sat there, eating and drinking, two members of the order were admitted to the chamber, and passed through into the room beyond.

Shortly after they had eaten and drunk their fill, San Thoy returned.

"I have spoken to Han Lay, Romojak of the order," he said, "and he and the brethren of this lodge have consented to admit you to our order, or, if you are unwilling to become members of the Chispoks, to permit you to depart in peace as you came."

"What are the requirements?" asked Grandon.

"You are to do all in your power to assist in the overthrow of the present regime in Huitsen," said San Thoy. "You are further to make solemn oath that you will render assistance to any brother Chispok in danger, even as you would have him render assistance unto you."

"I can see no objections to these requirements," replied Grandon. "In fact, I rather like the idea of assisting to overthrow the present regime, which certainly has not conducted itself in a friendly manner toward me. What say you, Gunner?"

"I would gladly become a Chispok, or even a sneaking ha-hoe, did Your Majesty recommend it," replied Kantar.

"Then lead on," Grandon told San Thoy. "The sooner we can become Chispoks, and get down to the real business at hand, the better."

Once more San Thoy gave three sharp raps at the door. It was flung open by a bowing yellow man, and they found themselves in a short, narrow hallway. At the other end of this, a second door opened at the same signal, and they entered a circular room about twenty-five feet in diameter. Squatting on low stone benches around the wall were about sixty Huitsenni. A man, older and more corpulent than the others, sat cross-legged on a dais in the center of the room. San Thoy conducted his two companions before this individual, introducing Grandon and Kantar as he had in the antechamber, to Han Lay, romojak of the lodge.

Han Lay rose, and bowed low before Grandon with right hand extended palm downward.

"The order of Chispoks is supremely honored," he said, "in that Your Imperial and Illustrious Majesty has consented to become one of us. We labor in a cause just now, which we have reason to believe is your own, and feel that with so mighty a fighter and so sagacious a general on our side, our cause is all but won."

"May I inquire to what cause you refer," asked Grandon, "and why you consider your cause my own?"

"We Chispoks have spies everywhere," replied Han Lay. "We are at present, endeavoring to overthrow Yin Yin, Rogo of Huitsen. Our spies inform us that he has not only kidnapped Her Majesty, your wife, for the purpose of selling her into slavery, but that, during the time she is to be kept in this city, he intends forcing her into his own seraglio."

"What!" Grandon's face went deathly pale, and upon his features there came a look which made even the brave Kantar feel anxious. Only twice before had he seen that look on the face of the Earth-man, and each time enemies had fallen before his flashing blade like frella grass at harvest.

"If you will but take me within sight of this filthy beast you call Yin Yin," said Grandon, "I will pierce his putrid heart, even though a thousand guardsmen surround him."

Han Lay grinned.

"That, Your Majesty, is precisely what we intend that you shall do," he said. "The Rogo of Huitsen is so strongly guarded that none of our assassins has been able to reach him, but we have every faith in your ability. When you have sworn the oaths of our order, the brothers will conduct you to the palace. Others will smuggle you into a chamber where, sooner or later, you will meet Yin Yin, face to face."

"Administer the oath quickly, then," replied Grandon, "that I may be on my way."

Kneeling, and with their right hands extended, palms downward, toward a small image of Thorth, which Han Lay held up before them, Grandon and Kantar swore the secret and terrible oath of the Chispoks.

The oath concluded, they arose, and the brethren crowded around them to extend fraternal greetings. But at this moment there came a sudden and unexpected interruption. One of the metal doors was thrown violently open, and a mojak with scarbo in hand and tork elevated to cover the group, burst into the room, followed by a horde of armed warriors.

The Chispoks were unarmed, save for their knives, hence at the mercy of the fully armed invaders, all of whom had torks and scarbos.

"You are all under arrest for treason against His Majesty, Yin Yin of Huitsen," proclaimed the mojak. "Throw down your knives and advance, one at a time, to have your wrists bound. Resist, and you are dead men."

Grandon noticed that Han Lay was edging toward a metal rod which projected through the floor of the dais. A moment later he stepped on it. There followed a sudden roar of rushing waters, which, in a brief instant engulfed both the Chispoks and the Rogo's men, and filled the room to the ceiling. Choking and strangling, Grandon was swept off his feet. Then his head collided with something hard and metallic, and he lost consciousness.

C H A P T E R XII

IN THE SERAGLIO

AFTER THE TWO GUARDS LED VERNIA from the presence of Yin Yin, they conducted her through a series of hallways to a spiral ramp, which they forced her to climb to a height of what she judged to be about six stories above the floor level of the throne room. Here, after threading several more hallways, they came to a metal door, on either side of which stood a tall, thin yellow man leaning on an immense scarbo. These were the first thin Huitsenni she had ever seen, and the sight astounded her, for she had believed that all of them, both men and women, were short and corpulent.

As Vernia and her two guards came to a stop before the door, one of those who stood beside it tapped on its metal surface with the hilt of his huge scarbo. It was instantly flung open, and a yellow man, taller than those who stood beside the door, and so aged that his face was a network of wrinkles, stood before them. He wore the purple cincture, showing that he was of the nobility, and his accouterments blazed with jewels. Seeing that Vernia wore the scarlet of royalty, he bowed low with right hand extended palm downward. Then he addressed the guard on her left.

"Whom have we here, and what are the commands?"

"O, Ho Sen, Lord of the Seraglio, this is Vernia, Torroga of Reabon. It is the command of His Majesty that Ufa be instructed to prepare her this night for the royal visit, for it may be that our gracious sovereign will honor her with the light of his presence."

"His Majesty is merciful, just and generous, and we delight to do his bidding," responded Ho Sen. Then he clapped his hands, and two more tall, slender Huitsenni came forward. They took the place of the two warriors who stood beside her, and the latter turned and marched off down the hall.

"Enter, Your Majesty," Ho Sen invited with a ceremonious bow. The strangely angular creatures at Vernia's sides seized her arms to drag her forward. But she shook them off and entered, herself. There was nothing else to do. Then the metal door clanged shut behind her.

Ho Sen led the way across this room through another oval entrance, and down a hallway into an immense chamber two stories in height, and shaped like a crescent, the far end of which was visible from where they stood. On the inner side of the crescent, numerous doors led out to little balconies which evidently overlooked the throne room, for Vernia could see the iridescent crystal walls of the immense shaft beyond. On the outer side of the crescent other doors led to sleeping apartments.

In the immense room were gathered no less than a thousand girls and young women. Among them were represented all the races of Zorovia with which Vernia was familiar, and several of which she had never heard. It was notable, too, that every girl, judged by the standards of her race, was beautiful.

Save for the tall, lean guards who stood at the doorways, and at regular intervals around the walls, there were no men present, and Vernia was beginning to suspect that even these were not men. Young slave girls padded softly about on the thick rugs, carrying trays of sweetmeats, pots and tiny bowls of kova, jars and bottles of cosmetics, combs, brushes, bangles, and such other feminine odds and ends as the pampered inmates of the seraglio required. Birds sang in gold and crystal cages that swung from the ceiling, and fountains splashed musically into limpid pools in which swam curious, brilliantly colored fish of many shapes and hues. In lieu of flowers, for such things are unknown on Zorovia, there were potted fungi of ornate shapes and rich shades, which filled the air with sweet, heavy perfume. These fungi, Vernia afterward learned, had been brought to their present state of perfection through careful selective breeding and crossing by hundreds of generations of skilled botanists. There were also many rare and beautiful varieties of ferns, cycads, and jointed grasses.

Many of the inmates lolled about on low divans, chatting, sipping kova, and nibbling at sweetmeats. Others were having their hair combed, their nails polished, or cosmetics applied by slave girls. A few were stringing beads or doing embroidery work, and the remainder strolled about the place or gathered in little groups, laughing and talking.

With a pompous dignity which showed that he took considerable pride in the grave responsibility reposed in him by the Rogo, Ho Sen picked his way among the divans, ottomans, fountains potted plants, and concubines, while Vernia, following with her two guards, felt as if on parade. It was plain to her that she was immediately the center toward which all eyes gravitated, as well as the subject of many remarks and dis-

cussions. The various members of this assorted aggregation
of feminine pulchritude showed different reactions as Vernia,
who was far more beautiful than any of them, passed. Some
gazed in open admiration, some cast lowering glances that
plainly denoted jealousy, others appeared coldly indifferent,
and a small remainder, evidently mindful of the fate intended
for her, looked sympathetic. Accustomed to being stared at,
she passed among them with easy grace and quiet dignity,
ignoring them as completely as if they had been so many articles
of furniture. But she could not help overhearing what some
of them said. Many exclaimed at her beauty. Others, the
jealous ones, made spiteful remarks. And she heard one girl
say: "Another princess, and as great a beauty as the first. It
seems that the Rogo has lately spread his nets for naught but
royalty."

Having passed about half way around the crescent, Ho Sen
led Vernia into a private suite, where a young girl sat having
her hair done by an old and extremely ugly yellow woman. The
girl, she noticed, wore the scarlet of royalty. She was small,
shapely, black-haired and brown-eyed.

Ho Sen addressed the old woman.

"I bring another great lady for your ministrations, Ufa.
She is Vernia, Torroga of Reabon. It is the will of His Majesty that she be prepared for the royal visit this night."

The old trot grinned. "We all love and obey our generous
and gracious sovereign," she replied, "and Ufa will exert herself to the utmost that this damsel may be pleasing to his
Majesty's eyes; though, in truth, her natural beauty makes the
task an easy one."

Ho Sen went out, closing the door after him.

The old hag grinned hideously at Vernia.

"Be seated, my pretty one," she said, "until I have finished
with my little white bird."

Vernia seated herself on a nearby divan, and a young slave
girl brought her a steaming pot of kova and a tiny golden

drinking bowl, which she placed near her on a small taboret. The girl who was having her hair done smiled and spoke to her.

"I am Narine of Tyrhana, Your Majesty," she said, "and, like you, a prisoner here. Shall we be friends? I've heard so much about your remarkable adventures, and your gallant husband, Grandon of Terra, that I feel as if I almost know you."

Vernia returned her friendly smile. "I who am friendless in this place," she replied, "would welcome the chance to acquire almost any friend, but in any case, I should be glad for the friendship of the daughter of Ad of Tyrhana, comrade of my father on many of his adventurous hunting excursions, his staunch ally when seven great nations combined and sought to break the naval power of Reabon, and now the ally of my husband. You are the Torrogina?"

"No, I am but the Torrogini. My elder sister, Loralie, is the Crown Princess. Perhaps you have heard of her engagement to Zinlo, Torrogo of Olba."

"I have. He visited Grandon of Terra a short time ago, and told us about their romance, but he did not mention that she was the Torrogina. You know they both traveled to this planet from Mignor at the same time, Grandon alighting in Uxpo, and Zinlo, who on Mignor was known as Harry Thorne, in Olba. But tell me, how do you happen to be here? Can it be that some lascivious torrogo has offered the price of an empire for your abduction?"

"I think not, as I expect to be sold into slavery today to the Rogo of the White Ibbits, a race of hairy barbarians who inhabit the Mountains of Eternal Snow near the south pole. It seems that Yin Yin buys large quantities of zandars from this savage chieftain, and that the latter has a weakness for comely virgins. Yin Yin has kept me here, unharmed, for the past ten days, for the sole reason that he believes I will bring him a tremendous price in zandars from this antarctic ruler.

"But you asked how I happened to be here. About an endir ago I left Tyrhana in one of my father's battleships to visit my cousin, Tinia, daughter of Aardvan of Adonijar. Three days out, a tremendous storm came up, carrying our masts and sails and more than half the crew overboard, destroying the steering apparatus and nearly filling the hold with water. In this helpless condition we drifted for many days. Then we sighted a fleet of pirate vessels. After a brief skirmish with the few warriors who were left behind on our ship, they boarded us and took all who remained alive prisoners. I was brought here, either to be sold or impressed into the seraglio of Yin Yin. He has seen fit to offer me to the barbarian for a fabulous number of zandars. I have sought to bribe Yin Yin to return me to my father, but he would not. Perhaps I can bribe the hairy chieftain. If not, why then I will die by my own hand, for the women of Tyrhana have ever preferred death to dishonor."

Vernia, in her turn, related what had befallen her since her capture by the Huitsenni.

In the meantime, Ufa finished with Narine's coiffure. Then she conducted Vernia into a magnificent bath of black and yellow marble, where she bathed in scented water, and was massaged with aromatic oils by two slave girls under the supervision of the efficient Ufa. After this, another slave girl brought splendid garments suited to her rank, and helped her to dress.

Back in the boudoir, Vernia had her hair done by Ufa. Presently Narine came in, and slave girls brought their evening meal. The repast was a sumptuous one, consisting of nearly a hundred tastily prepared dishes, from which they chose what they wanted. The napery was of scarlet silk, each piece embroidered with the coat of arms of the Rogo of Huitsen, and the service was of gold, similarly decked.

After they had dined, Ufa led them to another, larger room, the reception room of the suite, where a slave girl served them with kova. Then she departed, leaving them to their own devices.

With Ufa and the other slaves about, Vernia had kept the thought which was uppermost in her mind, escape, entirely out of the conversation. But now that she and Princess Narine were alone, she hoped that the Tyrhanian princess, having been in Huitsen for some time, might have acquired some knowledge which they could turn to their purpose.

"Don't you think," she said, as Narine filled her jeweled cup with steaming kova, "that you, with the wealth of Tyrhana behind you, could find someone in this palace, who, for a promise of vast riches, would smuggle us away in a small boat? Once at sea, we should be almost certain to encounter one of the many ships that must, by now, be searching for both of us."

Narine sipped her kova thoughtfully. "I have tried that," she replied, "and everywhere met with rebuffs. Every person I have tried to bribe has informed against me, and Yin Yin lost no time in letting me know that I was only wasting my breath."

"Can it be," asked Vernia, "that these people so love their tyrannous Rogo that not one of them would betray him for the wealth of an empire?"

"On the contrary," Narine replied, "I believe that every subject, from the most exalted noble to the lowest slave, fears and hates him. Yet no man dares speak his mind, for fear his fellow is a spy, or will turn informer to further his own ends."

"What of the man who has charge of the seraglio? Ho Sen, I believed they called him."

"The man, did you say?" Narine smiled. "Ho Sen is no man, but like these other angular creatures who stand about leaning on huge scarbos, is but a eunuch."

"A eunuch wearing the purple? That is strange. And I noticed that none of them were short and fat like the Huitsenni, although otherwise resembling them."

"They are all sons of slave women, mostly of the white races, so Ufa told me," Narine replied. "Some of them, I understand, are Yin Yin's own sons. Ho Sen is Yin Yin's uncle, though the Rogo does not acknowledge the relationship, and was granted the purple by Yin Yin's grandfather. He has been Lord of the Seraglio for three generations of royalty."

"Indeed! And does he love these yellow rulers who are the cause of his affliction and that of his fellows, so well that he could not be bribed to serve us?"

"I doubt that he loves his master any more than the others, yet I could not bribe him. I tried the first day I was brought here."

"Then there is no way we can help ourselves?"

"There is but one," replied Narine. "It is a desperate way, to be put into practice only as a last resort. But it is efficient. Look."

She twisted a blood-red jewel from a ring on her finger, and Vernia saw a few white crystals reposing in a tiny hollow beneath it.

"One of these crystals dissolved on the tongue brings death, sudden, sure, and painless," Narine told her. Then as she returned the jewel to its place, she said: "Yin Yin is careful to keep all weapons out of the seraglio with the exception of huge scarbos carried by the eunuchs. If he but knew the secret of this ring, then would my last hope indeed be gone."

"I, too, have managed to preserve the means to a quick way out, if worse comes to worst." Vernia drew a small, keen knife from beneath her garments and held it up. "This is from the belt of one of the guards who brought me to the seraglio. I managed to transfer it to these clothes after my bath, but it was difficult with the old hag and the slave girls watching."

Scarcely had she spoken, when there was a slight rustle of the hangings behind her. Then a fat, heavily jeweled hand reached over her shoulder and snatched the knife from her, and Yin Yin himself with a wheezy chuckle, waddled into the room. Still chuckling, and before she could prevent him, he seized Narine's slender wrist, and twisted the ring with the blood-red jewel from her finger. Then he dropped both articles into his belt pouch, poured himself a cup of kova, and sat down heavily.

"My, my!" he whispered, grinning toothlessly. "What desperate characters we have been entertaining unawares! Poison! Weapons! Bribery! I'm surprised. I'm astounded. I'm shocked."

He tossed off his kova and refilled the jeweled cup.

Narine said nothing, but there was a look of horror in her brown eyes.

Vernia, calm mistress of emotions, regarded him with regal hauteur. "I perceive," she said, addressing Narine, "that the Rogo of Huitsen has a multitude of low occupations. Not content with being a mere thief, robber, and defiler of womanhood, he is also that most contemptible of creatures, a spy."

Yin Yin set down his cup with a grunt of surprise, and his cat-like eyes narrowed. "Have a care, slave, how you speak of your master," he snarled, "or he may decide to have you whipped."

Still looking at Narine, Vernia replied. "Observe, Your Highness, how manly and chivalrous is the Rogo of Huitsen. Ah, what a different song he will sing when Grandon of Terra has him by the throat! He has a throat, I am sure, though it is concealed beneath his multiplicity of chins."

"It may be, Your Majesty," replied Narine, taking the cue, "that he has a throat, but is ashamed of it."

"Or what is more likely, Your Highness," Vernia responded, "he is afraid some honest man will slit it."

Yin Yin, arrayed in all his finery, had come to play the lover. But the most ardent wooer can seldom withstand ridicule, and if he be short-tempered and accustomed to having his every wish regarded as law, it is more likely that anger will quickly crowd the gentler passions from his bosom. Knowing this, Vernia had deliberately set out to bait him. It was evident, at first, that she had succeeded even beyond her expectations, for the bloated face of the monarch grew livid. A greenish glitter came to his cat-like eyes, and he muttered horrible threats. But Yin Yin, although gross and sensual, was a master of intrigue and an adept in cunning. And not many moments elapsed before he saw through the ruse. Suddenly he ceased his muttering and began laughing uproariously— laughing until the tears coursed down his puffy cheeks. After all, was he not complete master of the situation? And mere words, no matter what their burden, could not injure him.

With a pudgy finger he wiped the tears from his cheeks. Then he gulped down his kova, replaced the cup on the taboret, and shook that same fat finger at Vernia.

"Bones of Thorth, but you will be the death of me yet with your subtle humor," he wheezed. "A wittier pair of young ladies I have not seen in many a year—I who see thousands yearly, who come and go with the seasons."

From that moment on, he retained his good humor, nor could they with their keenest sallies or deepest insults penetrate the armor of jollity which he had assumed. A greasy, pleasure-bloated, jewel-bedizened monstrosity, he sat there, chuckling, boasting, and drinking cup after cup of steaming kova until the pot was empty and a slave girl was summoned with more.

The girl had just departed when there was the thunder of many hoofs on the planking of the street below. Yin Yin, with a maudlin smirk, addressed Narine. "If the Torrogini of Tyrhana will look over the balcony," he said, "it is possible that she will catch a glimpse of her future master. My ears tell me that Heg, Rogo of the Ibbits, has arrived with his savage riders, and ten thousand zandars for which I have offered to forego the pleasure of taming that little she-marmelot, the daughter of Ad of Tyrhana."

Both girls rushed to the nearest window, and stepping out on the balcony peered over. In the courtyard below them was an immense concourse of riders, mounted on zandars, wearing cloaks and hoods of zandar skins, and carrying long lances in their hands. But such lances! Each had about fifteen feet of stout wooden shaft, and a spiral head about two feet in length, connected to a globular metal knob. Vernia, herself a leader of warriors, was puzzled as to how these strange lances could be used, as it appeared that the spiral heads, instead of penetrating deeply when thrust at an enemy, would only spring back at the arm that drove them. The riders also carried scarbos and knives, but she saw no torks or evidence of firearms of any kind.

The faces and bodies of the riders were so muffled in their hoods and cloaks as to be invisible from above. The majority kept to their saddles, but about twenty of them dismounted and entered the palace. And looking out beyond the courtyard, Vernia saw by the light of the street lamps that an entire street, reaching from the palace to one of the city gates, was filled by an immense herd of milling, bellowing zandars, kept in formation by mounted Ibbits who prodded the recalcitrant beasts with the butts of their queer, spiral-pointed lances.

Turning away from the balcony, the two girls re-entered the room. Yin Yin, now evidently well under the influence of the kova he had consumed, was mumbling kerra spores and expectorating the red juice into one of the sand jars. His multiple chins stood much in need of the attentions of the royal chin-wiper, but he seemed too far gone in drink to notice this detail. He looked up suddenly as three sharp raps sounded at a side door.

"Come," he said, thickly.

Ho Sen, Lord of the Seraglio, entered, and bowed low with right hand extended palm downward.

"Your Majesty," he said, "Heg, Rogo of the Ibbits, has arrived, and awaits your pleasure at the outer door of the seraglio."

"Send him here by way of the single corridor, and see that two eunuchs attend him to this door," Yin Yin commanded. "There let him wait within call. It may be that this barbarian, when confronted with so much beauty at one time, will become difficult to manage."

"I hasten to obey," replied Ho Sen, with another bow and departed.

A few moments later the same door opened, and there entered a being who elicited from Vernia an involuntary gasp of amazement. With his hood of zandar thrown back and his great cloak of the same material caught at his shoulders, Heg, Rogo of the Ibbits, was a most remarkable sight. He was tall, towering head and shoulders above Yin Yin, and symmetrically built so far as human standards go, with the exception of his arms, which were not only tremendously muscled, but as long as those of an ape. His features, too, were regular, and his teeth even and white. Save for his scarlet cincture, and the gold and jewel studded straps which supported his knife and scarbo, he wore no clothing beneath his cloak, nor did he appear to need any. For his entire body, from head to foot, not excepting his whole face, was covered with short, white fur.

Yin Yin rose, as is the universal custom in Zorovia when royalty receives royalty, and the two exchanged salutations with right hands extended palms downward. Then he ceremoniously presented the savage chieftain to "Her Imperial Majesty, Vernia, Torroga of Reabon," and "Her Imperial Highness, Narine, Torrogini of Tyrhana." Neither Vernia nor Narine acknowledged the introduction, but this seemed to make no difference to the two rulers, who promptly seated themselves beside the taboret.

Yin Yin poured kova for himself and his guest, and they drank. Then he said: "Well, Heg, have you brought the zandars?"

"Aye, Yin Yin," was the reply. "Ten thousand of the most powerful and spirited beasts in my rogat are even now pawing the planks of your city in charge of my best herdsmen."

"You are satisfied with the bargain?"

Heg looked at Narine appraisingly. She shuddered under his gaze, but this did not seem to impress him. He had evidently seen many other maidens similarly frightened.

"I am quite satisfied, Yin Yin," he answered. "Come, look at the splendid zandars I have brought you, and see if you can find it in your heart to tell me that you are not pleased."

He rose, and led the way to the balcony, Yin Yin waddling after him.

"What think you of those beasts?" he asked. "And all for one little slave girl."

Yin Yin rubbed his pudgy hands together as the two turned away from the balcony and stepped back into the room. "They are indeed fine animals," he admitted, "and I declare myself satisfied, but speak not disparagingly of the little slave girl. Remember, she is the daughter of a mighty torrogo, and it cost me many men and much treasure to bring her here. Moreover, she has beauty far above the average."

"What of this other?" asked Heg, as they sat down once more beside the kova. "She also has great beauty, and I would buy her from you. In fact, each of these reaches the pinnacle of beauty for her type, the one brunette and the other blonde."

"Your taste in feminine charms is admirable," said Yin Yin, "as well it may be, seeing the number of famous beauties you have had from me. But you have always stipulated maids, and she of the golden curls is the bride of a torrogo, as you may have surmised from her title."

"Maid or matron, I care not. For beauty such as hers, I will break my rule. Ten thousand zandars more will be yours, magnificent as those I have brought you, in exchange for the golden-haired one."

"Nay, Heg. She is not for sale. All the zandars in your rogat, or all the countless millions that roam the antarctic wastes could not buy her, for she has already been sold for the value of a dozen kingdoms. It but remains for me to deliver her and collect my price."

But Heg was not easily turned from his purpose. Having seen Vernia, he meant to have her, arguing, threatening, pleading, and gradually increasing his offers, while the two drank cup after cup and pot after pot of kova. He at length avowed his willingness to fill all the streets of Huitsen, packed solidly to the doorways, with zandars, if Yin Yin would only sell him this delectable bit of femininity that, as he expressed it, he might turn at will from the dark beauty of the one to the blonde glory of the other.

Meanwhile the two girls, who had retired to a corner of the room, whispered together.

"Never in my wildest fancies," said Vernia, "did I ever dream that I should become the subject of such haggling as this—to be sold, offered for sale, or bidden for, like a beast of burden."

"It all seems like a wild nightmare, too horrible to be real," replied Narine. "Think of it! I have been sold by a greasy rodent to a fur-covered savage—I the daughter of Ad of Tyrhana! Oh that I had kept the secret of the ring intact! Now I fear that death will come too late to save my honor."

"My deepest regret is that I, too, betrayed my secret by displaying my knife. I could at least have had the pleasure of sheathing it in the foul heart of Yin Yin before employing it to still for ever the beating of my own. I have but one hope on which to lean, and that is a slender one. Grandon of Terra is free somewhere in this city, or was when I last heard of him. Though he and Kantar the Gunner, his friend and warrior, were unarmed, they may have found a way to obtain weapons. If so, it will take more guards than Yin Yin possesses to keep them from the palace, for they must know that I have been brought here."

"It is indeed a slender hope," sighed Narine; "for even though your gallant husband could win his way to this place, there would be no way out. It would be but a death trap for all of us."

"In that case," Vernia replied, "I should die contented, for there would be hordes of enemies to accompany us into the great beyond and stand before the judgement throne of Thorth."

As the two Rogos reached an advanced state of inebriation, their haggling became louder and louder, until it appeared that a quarrel was iminent. Suddenly, the hand of the savage chieftain flew to the hilt of his scarbo, and he sprang to his feet, overturning a taboret. "Sell me this fair-haired beauty, and name your own price," he shouted, "but sell her to me you shall, or by the blood of Thorth I'll slay you and take her for nothing."

Yin Yin looked at him in drunken wonderment for a moment, as if he could not believe his own eyes. Then he clapped his hands. Instantly the door through which the hairy one had come, flew open, and two eunuchs ran into the room, bared blades in their hands.

At this, Heg's bravado instantly subsided. Letting his furry hand drop from his hilt, he said: "What's this? You call the guard? I did but jest, my friend." "Your jest, as you call it, has gone far enough," wheezed Yin Yin. "We will, however, let it pass as such, and so end the conference. Take your slave girl and be gone, for the torroga of Reabon and I would be alone." He turned his cat-like eyes on Vernia, and leered drunkenly. "Wouldn't we, my pretty?"

"It grows late, and I must indeed be going," replied Heg. Striding across the room, he suddenly seized Narine's wrist and jerked her to her feet. She screamed, and attempted to free her arm from his brutal grasp, but he only laughed at her struggles. "Come, my little beauty," he said, dragging her across the room. "We have outworn our welcome."

One of the eunuchs held the door open, and the other stood aside from them to pass out. Yin Yin, a kerra-stained grin on his porcine features, rose ponderously, and waddled unsteadily toward Vernia, drunkenly oblivious to her expression of fear and loathing.

C H A P T E R   XIII

GRANDON MEETS THE ROGO

AFTER GRANDON STRUCK HIS HEAD AND
lost consciousness in the water-filled lodge room of the Chispoks, his senses returned slowly. At first it seemed that he
was in a vast hall—that a gigantic figure was bending over
him, shouting something which he could hear only as a faint
sound in the distance, and that other immense figures were
moving about the room.

But gradually, as he became more rational, the room and
everything in it assumed their proper proportions. He saw
that he was lying on a sleeping shelf in a room much smaller
than that in which he had lost consciousness, and that the
supposed giant was Kantar the Gunner, leaning over him.

The other occupants of the room were Han Lay, San Thoy, and a half dozen Chispoks.

"Speak to me, Majesty," Kantar was saying. "Only let me know that you—"

"I'm all right, Gunner. Let me up." With the astounded and delighted Kantar's arm beneath his shoulders, he sat up. His head swam dizzily, but gradually it cleared. "Where are we?" he asked.

Han Lay, who had hurried to his bedside as soon as he saw him sit up, bowed and said: "Perhaps I can explain better than the warrior, Your Majesty. You recall that we were attacked by the Rogo's soldiers in the lodge room?"

"I remember that, and the flood afterward. Then I must have struck my head for all went black."

"I tried to help you," continued Han Lay, "but as you were not expecting the sudden rush of waters you were swept off your feet and carried away before I could reach you. Your head collided with the end of a doorway. All the Chispoks, of course, knew how to get out, for we had rehearsed it many times. San Thoy helped your warrior to escape through the secret door, and I dragged you out the same way. The last man out closed it."

"Then the Rogo's warriors did not escape?"

"Not one man. But of course it was necessary for us to destroy the building, for there will be an investigation, and we have other buildings similarly equipped. All this was prepared for in advance. The pulling of a lever in this house set off a tremendous charge of explosive which blew the place to atoms. We brought you here to my home, in my boat."

Grandon stood up to test the strength of his legs. Although the dizziness assailed him for a second time, he was able to stay on his feet.

"Permit me to thank you for saving my life," he said. "It may be that some day I shall find a way to repay you."

"You can best repay me by carrying out the plans we outlined before you took the oath of our fraternity."

"I'll gladly do that, and more," replied Grandon. "Give me my instructions, and let me start."

"You will have little to do until the brothers who will smuggle you into the palace bring you face to face with Yin Yin. If you succeed in slaying him and rescuing Her Majesty, your wife, the Chispoks will not only guarantee to help you escape from the palace by the way you entered, but will further promise to conduct you out of Huitsen and place you aboard a seaworthy craft on the Azpok, with provisions and water sufficient to last you until you reach the shores of your own land. Is this agreeable?"

"Perfectly," Grandon replied. "But I would be fair with you as you have been with us. What of the secret way into Huitsen which I and my warrior now know? Would you expect us to keep this secret from the rest of Zorovia, in spite of the relentless raids and acts of outlawry which will no doubt continue to be perpetrated by your people?"

"We have provided against that, also," replied Han Lay, "for we are aware that any one of the twelve great nations of Zorovia, knowing where we are, could easily wipe out Huitsen. However, permit me to point out that, even though you saw the secret passageway and how it was operated, you were not navigating the ship; hence you have no idea just where it is. You saw that the entrance was through a fiord, but there are countless thousands of fiords on this coast, many of which look like this one. All we will need to do will be to blindfold you and those who are to go with you, until you are at sea and out of sight of land. The brothers will then direct you how to sail to reach your own country, but you will not be able to find our particular fiord again in many years of careful searching, unless it be by accident or unusual good luck.

"I might say, further, that in the event of the Chispoks succeeding to the point of taking over the government, piracy will be stopped, peace treaties will be signed with all the great nations of Zorovia, and Huitsen will be thrown open to the ships of the world. It was for this principle that the Chispoks were organized. The Huitsenni have been pirates for countless generations. Once our nation was as great and powerful as any on Zorovia, but now we are among the least of powers. Why? The Chispoks hold that commerce has made other nations greater than our own. By the very nature of our livelihood we are debarred from peaceful trading, or commerce of any kind with the exception of an occasional kidnapping for some lascivious ruler, infrequent ransom money for wealthy or influential people captured on the high seas, and the little we can get for our plunder in trade and goods from these shady and grasping merchants who run the double risk of dealing with us—first because they fear we may betray them, and second because they may be apprehended and punished by their own people. Naturally they exact exorbitant profits, and our ill-gotten plunder never brings us a tenth of its real worth in exchange.

"The Chispoks are sick of piracy, of this secret slinking from the sight of other nations as the hahoe slinks from the path of the mighty marmelot. We are weary of the constant bloodshed which is a part of our trade. And it is our ambition to place Huitsen on a peaceful footing with all Zorovia, to turn our pirate vessels into merchantmen, to have our people received with friendship and good will whenever they set foot on a foreign shore."

"A worthy ambition, and I'll do all I can to further it," said Grandon.

"Good. And now do you feel strong enough to leave for the palace?"

"Perfectly."

Han Lay led Grandon and Kantar to his private arsenal, from which each selected a scarbo, knife, tork, and ammunition. When both were armed he walked with them to the door, and said: "The six brothers here will take you to the palace. They have instructions, and you may trust them implicitly."

Looking out, Grandon saw that the six Chispoks, attired as fishermen, were standing in a semicircle, which screened the door and the fishing hole beside it, from view.

"Crouch behind the men and descend the ladder," Han Lay said. "There are two boats moored. Each of you is to get into one and wrap himself in a fishing net. Farewell, and may Thorth guide and keep you."

Grandon did as directed, and Kantar followed close behind him. Scarcely had they established themselves in the boats, when three pseudo-fishermen descended into each, and rowed away.

Lying in the bottom of the boat, looking up through the meshes of the net, Grandon could see but little. The light from the street lamps shone faintly through the interstices in the planking above his head, and by means of it he could barely make out the outlines of piling and the foundations of the buildings they passed. At times the rowers saluted, and were saluted by the crews of other small fishing boats, but otherwise they maintained unbroken silence.

Presently Grandon saw an immense stone foundation looming ahead of them, and stretching to the right and left farther than he could see, in so wide an arc that he knew it must be the base of some tremendous building. Then the prow of the boat in which he rode slid up on a low dock. A moment later he heard another prow grind up beside it. Then one of the pseudo-fishermen spoke.

"Greetings, thalput of the royal kitchens."

"Greetings, fishermen," was the reply. "Have you brought the fish, as ordered?"

"The fish are here in the nets."

"Then bring them, and follow me."

Still wrapped in the net, Grandon was swung up to the shoulders of the three men, who walked across a low dock and entered a large oval door. After following a dimly lighted passageway for some distance, they suddenly turned aside into a narrow doorway. A moment later, the other three strode in after them, and the door was softly closed. Grandon was set on his feet, and the folds of the net were unwound from his body. As soon as Kantar was similarly freed, the six fishermen took their nets and departed, closing the door after them.

They were in a tiny room, faintly lighted by a single dim bulb that shone from the center of the ceiling. The place had metal walls and was bare of furniture. No outlet was visible save the door through which they had come. But he who had been addressed as the kitchen thalput, pressed one of a row of studs, whereupon a panel slid back, revealing the bottom of a narrow spiral stairway, as dimly lighted as the room in which they stood.

"Follow me," he whispered, "and make no sound. Take care that your weapons do not clink against the walls."

As soon as Grandon and Kantar had stepped inside, the thalput pressed a stud, and the panel closed behind them. Then he led the way up the spiral stairway. At intervals of about fifteen feet thereafter, they passed sliding panels, above each of which was fastened a dim bulb. When they had reached the ninth panel, the thalput stopped before it. He pressed a stud, and the panel slid back, revealing a dark opening behind scarlet hangings. From behind these came the sound of spirited haggling. The thalput pressed a lower stud, and the panel slid back once more without a sound, shutting off the noise of voices beyond. Then he addressed Grandon:

"In yonder room," he said, "you will find Her Majesty, your wife, the Rogo of Huitsen, and the Rogo of the Ibbits. I gather from the conversation that the savage chieftain is trying to persuade Yin Yin to sell your wife to him. I leave you

here to lay your plans as may seem best to you. If you succeed, you will find me at the foot of the steps, and the boats
and fishermen will be ready to convey you hence. Farewell,
brother Chispoks, and may Thorth guide your scarbos! Death
to the tyrant!"

As the thalput began his descent of the stair, Grandon said:
"My plans are made, Gunner, and I want you to carry out
your part as ordered, without giving heed to what may follow.
I will go in and engage those two drunken rogos in combat. It
will be your part to rescue my wife while I am so doing. My
positive instructions to you are that, no matter what odds I
may have to fight, no matter if you see me fall and at the
mercy of my enemies, you must not join in the fight. Instead
bend every effort toward rescuing Her Majesty. Convey her
down the stairway as soon as possible, and do not wait for
me. Take one of the boats, and be off immediately, to the
place of refuge which the Chispoks have prepared for us. If
I live I will follow. If not, our chief object will have been
accomplished—the rescue of my wife; and you will do your
best to get her safely back to Reabon Do you understand?"

"Perfectly. But to see Your Majesty go down and not—"

"What! I was under the impression that a soldier was with
me."

"But, Majesty—"

"A soldier obeys orders implicitly."

"Yes, Majesty."

"You will so obey."

"I will so obey, Majesty."

"Good. Wait here until you hear the clash of blades. Then
enter, and carry out your instructions to the letter."

"To the letter, Majesty."

Grandon pressed the upper stud and the panel slid open. A
woman's scream and a man's voice saying: "Come my little
beauty, we have outworn our welcome," spurred him to instant
action. Leaping through the panel, he flung the scarlet hang-

ings wide, and stepped into the room, bared blade in hand.

At a glance, he saw that he would have four swordsmen to contend with instead of two. One eunuch held a door open while another stood opposite him. A tall hairy fellow with a white fur cloak was dragging a pretty, brown-eyed girl toward the door. And the fat, greasy Rogo of Huitsen was waddling toward Vernia, grinning drunkenly.

At the sight of Grandon, Vernia cried: "Bob! My dearest I knew you would come!"

Yin Yin turned and whipped out his scarbo. Heg, Rogo of the Ibbits, dropped the arm of the brown-eyed girl, and also drew his blade, leaping toward Grandon. The two eunuchs caught up their heavy weapons and followed. There was a clash of steel on steel. Yin Yin parried once and struck once. Then his head flew from his shoulders, thudded to the floor, and rolled beneath the divan. For an instant the headless body stood there, blood spouting from the neck as from a fountain. Then it collapsed, a quivering mound of flabby flesh.

Grandon turned to face three blades. The brown-eyed princess, meanwhile, had run across the room to stand beside Vernia. Instead of waiting on guard, the Earth-man attacked with a brilliant display of that swordsmanship which had made him famous throughout all Zorovia. Before his fierce onslaught, the three gave way. His blade seemed to be everywhere at once, flashing with the speed of lightning.

Heg was disarmed, almost with the second slash he made at Grandon, his weapon flying behind a divan. But he leaped nimbly back, then drawing his knife, strove to encircle the Earth-man, evidently for the purpose of knifing him in the back. Grandon guessed his intention, but was now so beset by the two eunuchs with their long, two-handed scarbos, that he could give the hairy chieftain but scant attention. Once when he thought the savage Rogo was just behind him, he slashed back for an instant with his scarbo, but the blade encountered only empty air, and he came near having his head split open by the nearest eunuch. He stepped aside just in time, and as the heavy blade crashed to the floor, its wielder received a thrust in the throat and followed his master into the great beyond. With this fellow out of the way, Grandon quickly disposed of the other with a leg cut followed by a swift neck blow that sent the head of the slave to keep company with that of the master.

Whirling to face his furry enemy, Grandon was astounded to see that, save for himself and three corpses, the room was deserted. He instantly came to the conclusion that Kantar had rescued both Vernia and the strange, black-haired princess. But what, he wondered, had become of this furry fellow from the antarctic? Puzzled, he was about to return to the panel opening when he heard a cry—the voice of Vernia. "Bob! The window! Quickly!"

He leaped through the window, and peered over the balcony railing. Below him he saw the hairy chieftain dropping with ape-like agility from balcony to balcony, using one arm to swing himself down and holding Vernia with the other. The courtyard below was packed with furry warriors mounted on zandars. One saddled beast was being led to a point just under the lowest balcony.

Sheathing his bloody scarbo, and unmindful of the dizzy height, Grandon swung himself over the railing, and began dropping from balcony to balcony. But before he was half way down, the furry rogo was in the saddle, with Vernia, wrapped in a zandar cloak and swung across the bow. He gave a few swift orders, then galloped off. With the exception of one man, the entire cavalcade followed him. That man sat his mount beneath the lowest balcony, evidently left there to slay Grandon, for his long lance with its queer, corkscrew head was slightly pointed at the spot where the Earth-man would shortly alight.

C H A P T E R XIV

KANTAR'S BLUNDER

ALTHOUGH KANTAR, AS SOON AS HE FOL-
lowed Grandon through the panel opening, saw that his sovereign was beset by overwhelming odds, and would have liked
nothing better than to join in the swordplay, he was constrained
by the strict orders which the Earth-man had given him. His
part was to get Vernia out of the palace as quickly as possible.

Peering through the narrow slit between two hangings, he
saw the headless yellow body with a scarlet cincture, which
identified it as that of Yin Yin. Only a few inches in front of
him he noticed a jeweled hand and a slim, white arm. It did
not occur to him that there could be any woman other than
Vernia in the room. But the thought did come to him that
she would surely refuse to leave Grandon—that if he should

urge her to go she would undoubtedly countermand the positive instructions which had been given to him. He decided to carry her off, and explain afterward.

He thought he could tell precisely where she stood by the position of her hand and arm, and acted accordingly. Suddenly jerking the silken hanging from the bar on which it was draped, he wrapped it around the slender figure, and turning, plunged through the panel opening. Then, carrying his precious burden in his arms, he dashed down the winding stairway. Muffled sounds of terror came from the bundle, but he spoke reassuringly: "Be not afraid, Majesty. It is I, Kantar the Gunner. His Majesty ordered me to carry you hence quickly. Friends are waiting to help us out of the city."

The cries and struggles subsided, and Kantar quickly reached the bottom of the stairway. Here he found the thalput waiting as he had promised.

"Is Yin Yin dead?" he asked.

"His head and body just parted company," replied Kantar.

"Thorth be praised! The tyrant is no more! And his Majesty of Reabon?"

"Still fighting when I left. He ordered me to proceed without him, and said that on no account should I wait for him, but should take Her Majesty away from here at once."

"That scarcely comports with our plans, but he has earned the right to be obeyed by all Chispoks. And I'll be on the lookout to help him if he comes later. Follow me."

He opened the panel which led into the small metal-walled room, and there stood the six pseudo-fishermen with their nets. Swiftly they wrapped a net around Kantar's bundle, and another around the gunner. Then shouldering their burdens as before, they filed out into the passageway, the thalput at their heels.

Kantar heard someone coming, and wondered how the two full nets passing out of the palace would be explained. But the thalput was equal to the occasion.

"Take your stale fish and feed them to the ormfs," he cried in a loud voice, "and the next time you try to force such trash on the thalput of the royal kitchen, I'll see that His Majesty learns of it."

A moment later the two bundles were lowered into the boats, the rowers took their places, and the thalput pushed them off. For some time Kantar lay there looking up at the monotonous scenery of planking, piling, and stone foundations. They traversed a narrow passage between two stone walls, and shortly thereafter shot out under the sky. The gunner recognized the harbor of Huitsen.

A few strokes of the oars took them alongside an anchored boat about twenty-five feet long. It had a small, low cabin, and was fitted with two bat-wing sails. The two bundles were passed up to a stocky yellow man, who carried them, one at a time, into the cabin.

A dim light illuminated the little room, and as Kantar looked up at the man who deposited him there, he recognized San Thoy.

"Both of you must stay wrapped like this for some time," said the former mojak. "Where is Grandon of Terra?"

"Dead or alive, I know not," replied Kantar. "But he slew Yin Yin, and by his command I left him there, still fighting, to bring Her Majesty here."

"The fact that he slew Yin Yin places me doubly in his debt," said San Thoy. "We will wait here for him a while, but we must start in time to get out under cover of darkness, or I fear we shall not get out at all."

"By all means, wait as long as you dare," replied the loyal gunner, "but if he does not come in time, I know his desire would be that we should go on without him."

"I trust that you and Her Majesty will make yourselves as comfortable as possible while I go to keep watch on the deck. Under no circumstances must you make a noise or uncover yourselves. Yin Yin's warriors may board us at any time, and were they to discover our secret we should all die."

He went outside, and remained for some time in low conversation with the six men. Presently Kantar heard another boat come alongside, and scarcely dared to breath for fear it contained warriors.

There was the sound of some one coming up over the side, and whispering. Then San Thoy came into the cabin.

"It is useless to wait longer," he said. "A brother just came to inform us that Grandon of Terra is believed to have been carried off by the Ibbits; whether dead or alive, they know not. We will start."

"I'm sure that we will be carrying out his wishes by doing so," replied Kantar.

San Thoy went out on deck, and issued a few commands. The bat-wing sails were unfurled and the anchor hoisted. To accelerate their progress, for the wind was not strong here in the harbor, the men used oars, while San Thoy went forward to operate the steering device, which was shaped like an eight-pointed star with a knob on each point and suspended horizontally above the compass. The two rowboats in which the men had come were towed behind.

Presently Kantar knew by the disappearance of the breeze and the faint echoes which followed every sound, that they had entered the subterranean lake. A little later he heard a voice which seemed to come from above him.

"Ho, there. Who goes?"

"Gar Zin, the fisherman," replied San Thoy, "to catch a killer-norgal for the royal table."

"A moment, Gar Zin. It seems your voice has altered considerably. I'll just descend and have a closer look at you."

"As you please, Excellency," San Thoy replied with studied carelessness. "We'll have a bowl of kova in my cabin." He clapped his hands. "Ho, Lin Fan. Prepare kova in the cabin at once for His Excellency, Yin Fu, Guardian of the Gate."

One of the men hurried into the cabin. Peering through the meshes of his net, Kantar saw the man enter. But he did not approach the small fish-oil stove that was fastened to one wall. Instead, he crouched beside the door, a knife gleaming in his hand.

From outside came the squeak of pulleys and the thud of feet on the deck. Evidently some one had been lowered to the boat from a station high above it.

"Welcome to my humble ship, Excellency," said San Thoy.

"Umph. It is as I thought. You are not Gar Zin, my old friend. Who are you, and what are you up to?"

San Thoy asumed a confidential tone. "Shh! Not so loud, Excellency. Private business for his Majesty. Come into the cabin, and we'll discuss it over a bowl of kova."

"I'll come into the cabin, right enough, but I want none of your kova. Lead on."

"After you, Excellency."

"I said, lead on!" There was the sound of a scarbo being whipped from its sheath. "I'll keep this point at your back, and at the first sign of treachery, you die."

"As you wish, Excellency." San Thoy's tone was exceedingly humble.

Peering through the meshes, Kantar saw San Thoy enter the cabin, followed by a large yellow man who wore the purple cloak and shining helmet of conical shape. In his hand he carried a scarbo, the point of which was directed at San Thoy's back.

Just as Yin Fu stepped through the door, San Thoy threw himself face downward on the floor. At the same moment, a knife flashed from beside the door, and the guardian of the gate collapsed with a grunt of anguish.

San Thoy leaped to his feet. For a moment he bent and held his hand over the heart of the fallen noble. Then he removed the purple cloak and helmet, and donned them. Going out on deck, he shouted in excellent imitation Yin Fu's voice:

"It's all right, warriors. Open the gate. I'm going out with my old friend, Gar Zin, to drink a bowl or two with him, and have a try at norgal. Look well to your tasks until I return."

There followed a whirring of hidden machinery, and a sliding sound as of stone over metal. Then the rowers bent to their oars. San Thoy, meanwhile, discarded the helmet and cloak in the cabin, and hurried out to take his place on the steermen's seat. Soon the boat began rocking with considerable violence. Shortly thereafter the rowers ceased their efforts, and Kantar knew that they were now afloat on the open Azpok, and plunging forward under the impetus of a stiff breeze.

Presently San Thoy gave the steersman's seat to another, and entered the cabin. "We'll have to put out the light for awhile," he said. "They will use a glass on us from the shore, and we don't want them to know in which direction we are going. At least you will not have to stay trussed up in these nets any longer, and I can dispose of that," pointing to the corpse of Yin Fu. He looked around the cabin for a moment as if to fix the location of everything in his mind. Then he put out the light, and the gunner heard him dragging his grisly burden out of the cabin, heard a splash, and knew that the remains of Yin Fu had gone to feed the denizens of the Azpok.

Kantar quickly rolled out of his net, and went over to where his precious bundle lay. "If you don't mind, I'll help you out of this, Your Majesty," he said. "I'm sure you will be more comfortable."

"I'm sure I shall," was the reply. "You have been very kind."

The gunner was startled at the sound of the voice. It did not sound like that of Vernia. But he thought she might have taken cold from this unwonted exposure. Then, too, her voice would sound differently, muffled in the hanging.

"You have been very brave, Majesty," he replied, as he unwound the net. "Perhaps this silk around you will add to your comfort. The breeze is chill."

He adjusted the silken drape around the shapely shoulders.
A soft hand touched his, and thrilled him unaccountably. It
gave him rather a guilty feeling, that thrill, but he could no
more help it than he could help breathing.

"Ho, Gunner. Can you help me with the boat? The crew
is leaving."

"Coming, San Thoy," was the reply. He felt his way to
the door in the pitch blackness, then stepped out on deck. Outside it was fully as dark as in the cabin. Nothing whatever
was visible except the occasional glint of a star through a
rent in the ever-present cloud envelope.

A hand was laid on his arm. "Let me guide you," said San
Thoy, whose cat-like pupils enabled him to see by the faint
flashes of starlight. "Sit here, so, and take these ropes in your
hands. Now pull the right or left rope, or both, as I may
direct. I will steer."

"Where are the brothers?" asked Kantar.

"They were leaving when I called you. They will reach
the two boats, and return to Huitsen by a roundabout way
known only to the Chispoks."

"I trust that they will not lose their lives for this night's
work."

"There is little danger. Their part in the affair is not
known. Also, it is possible that the Chispoks may be in power
when they return."

"But what of you?"

"I will accompany you back to Reabon. In Huitsen I am
a fugitive, but in your country I feel that I shall be welcome
after this night's work. Later, if and when the Chispoks as-
sume control of Huitsen, I shall return."

"No one will be more welcome," replied the gunner, "unless
it be Grandon of Terra himself."

They sailed on and on into the moonless Zorovian night,
and Kantar, who was aware of the almost uncanny skill with

which the Huitsenni navigated their boats, did not doubt that they were heading in the right direction.

Presently San Thoy said: "We could have a light now, as we are out of sight from shore. But it is scarcely worth while, as morning will soon dawn."

A few moments later a faint blood-orange tint marked the outlines of the eastern horizon, swiftly followed by the full blaze of cloud-filtered morning light.

"There are provisions and kova in the cabin," said San Thoy. "Perhaps you will prepare breakfast for Her Majesty. It is best that I continue to steer for yet a while. The breeze is quite steady now, so you may lash the ropes."

"If my nose doesn't deceive me," replied the gunner, who was closer to the cabin than San Thoy, "breakfast is already being prepared. However, I'll go and assist."

Making the two ropes fast, he got up and went to the cabin. Pausing to make obeisance to his Torroga, he gasped in sudden astonishment at sight of a slender, dark-haired girl bending over the fish-oil burner, from the top of which came the fragrant aroma of brewing kova and the savory odor of a well-seasoned meat and mushroom stew. As the morning was chill, the girl still wore the silken curtain draped around her, concealing her garments but not the graceful lines of her slim body.

"Bones of Thorth!" he exclaimed. "Who are you?"

She looked up, her face slightly flushed by the heat from the stove, and Kantar gasped again; for never, he thought, had he seen a face so beautiful. At first her eyes flashed imperiously, almost angrily, at the abruptness and bluntness of his question. But suddenly the icy look melted, was replaced by a winning smile.

"My name is Narine," she replied. "And you, I believe, are Kantar the Gunner."

Kantar's wonder deepened. For a moment he was wholly under the spell of those big brown eyes. Then he remembered his duty—the trust with which his sovereign had charged him.

"Where is Her Majesty of Reabon?" he asked. "And how did you get on this boat?"

"Her Majesty," replied Narine, "was watching the brilliant swordplay of her valiant husband when I last saw her. As for your other question, who should know more about how I got here than you, who brought me?"

"I brought you!" His heart sank. "Then I have failed in my trust."

Instantly she saw the look of dejection on his face, and answered with one of sympathy.

"I'm sorry," she said. "I see now that there has been a dreadful mistake. Would that I had known this when you seized me there in the seraglio! Her Majesty had mentioned your name to me. We had planned to escape together. But naturally I did not know His Majesty's plans—or yours. When you told me your name and asked me to be quiet, I believed that it was your intention to rescue me—that Grandon of Terra would look out for his own."

"So he would, ordinarily," replied Kantar. "But he was sorely beset. My orders were to bring away his wife; to stay out of the fight for that sole purpose, no matter how the odds went against him. And I brought you!"

"I'm terribly sorry—" she began.

"Sorry! You should have known. Didn't I address you as 'Your Majesty'? Did not that tell you whom I believed I was carrying?"

"Truly it did not. I thought you had taken me for a torroga instead of— that is—"

"I take you for a torroga?" He laughed mirthlessly. "You, a mere slip of a girl?"

"I'm eighteen," she retorted.

"So? And what of it? I would never take you for a torroga."

For a moment the shadow of a smile hovered on her features. But it only angered him the more. He had made a mistake, a most horrible mistake which he felt that Grandon, if still alive, could never pardon—a mistake, moreover, for which he felt positive he could never forgive himself. A thousand fears assailed him. Torturing pictures flashed through his mind. Grandon dead, his head adorned a pike before the Ibbit palace, or if alive, a slave of the savage chieftain from the Mountains of Eternal Snow. Vernia the plaything of this barbarous rogo, or, if she had been left in the seraglio, of Yin Yin's successor! For a moment he struggled to master his unreasoning anger against this girl who had been the unwitting cause of his failure to keep trust. Then he said: "From what country do you hail?"

"From Tyrhana," she replied. "Won't you sit down at the table and let me serve you?"

"Why, yes," he answered. "I'll admit that I'm hungry, thirsty, and weary."

She set food and drink before him. He sipped his kova. "You brew an excellent bowl," he told her, and tasting his stew: "This food is not half bad."

She smiled. "The Tyrhanians are a maritime people," she replied, "and should know how to prepare seamen's rations."

"I forgot," he said. "San Thoy must be hungry. I'll take food and drink to him before I begin."

"No, let me. I've been resting all night, and I'll confess that I tasted the stew and the kova." She set the things on a tray and went out, while the gunner addressed himself to his provender. Presently she returned, poured herself a bowl of kova, and took a helping of stew. Then she sat down opposite him.

"A lovely morning," she remarked.

"Is it?" he replied, absently. "I've been thinking about you, wondering what I'm going to do with you."

"Indeed!"

"Yes. You see I haven't time to take you all the way to Tyrhana. I must go back to Huitsen, to do what I can to help their Majesties of Reabon, if indeed they are not beyond all human help."

"Perhaps I could get you some assistance from Tyrhana. You see," she suggested, "my father—that is—"

"No use," he replied. "Tyrhana is on the opposite side of the world. By the time we went there and returned—"

But Tyrhana has great fleets, even now, scouring every sea on the globe in search of—a lost princess."

"A lost princess!"

"Yes. Some time ago the Torrogini set sail in one of her father's battleships. She has not been heard from since. Naturaly, the Torrogo, who loves his daughters beyond all else, is bending every effort to find her."

"Naturally," replied Kantar. "But the chances are much against our meeting any of his ships on the broad Azpok."

"You forget," reminded Narine, "that Tyrhana has the mightiest navy on all Zorovia."

"Reabon has a navy second only to that of Tyrhana," replied Kantar, "and her ships are now scouring the Azpok; Yet I do not place much reliance on the chance of meeting any of them. Besides—"

He was interrupted by a shout from San Thoy. "Gunner. Bring the glass. I believe we are pursued."

Kantar snatched the spy-glass from the rack behind him, and hurried out on deck. He saw a ship coming from the southwest, and a sail looming above the southeast horizon. Quickly focusing the glass on the sail, he saw a lookout at the masthead, his glass trained directly on them. A glimpse at the other ship was sufficient to show him that they were being chased from this quarter. Even as he looked, two mattork crews were going into action on the forward deck. A moment later, a shell screamed overhead, and another exploded in the water about two hundred feet behind them.

"Poor marksmanship," he commented coolly. "But I suppose they'll get the range presently. Would that I had a mattork with which to reply!"

"We have two," said San Thoy, "one fore and one aft. Pull up the ring in the after-deck."

Kantar hurried back and did as requested. The square of the deck to which the ring was attached came up and tilted forward. It was plated beneath with metal, forming a bulletproof shield. And behind this shield there appeared a shiny new mattork, mounted on its tripod, with cases for the projectile clips and gas clips.

Quickly the gunner opened the breech, inserting a gas clip and a shell clip marked "explosive." There were other shell clips marked "solid," but for the present, he ignored these. Closing the breech, he knelt, and taking careful aim, pressed the firing button. One of the mattork crews on the approaching ship disappeared a moment later, as if by magic.

The shells from the other mattork, as well as from the heavier turret mattorks of the pursuing craft, were screaming around them in vast numbers, and kicking up tremendous geysers in the sea on all sides. He heard a voice at his side: "May I help you?" Turning, he looked in the wistful brown eyes of Narine. She did not appear to realize their danger, for there was no trace of fear in her expresion. "I can hand you the clips."

"Get back into the cabin, you little fool!" he told her. Not waiting to see if she would obey, he once more turned his attention to the enemy. A second well-placed shot wiped out the other mattork crew, and he noted with grim satisfaction that no more came out on the deck. Perhaps the pirates realized now with whom they had to deal. The heavier turret mattorks, though their projectiles could do incalculably greater damage, could not be aimed nearly so accurately as the lighter deck weapons such as he used.

By this time the other pirate ship was in full view. Evidently its commander had seen what happened on the other vessel, for he ordered out only one deck mattork crew. The gunner quickly obliterated it, and had the satisfaction of seeing that this commander, also, was wise enough to use only his turret mattorks thereafter.

"Splendid shooting." Again he heard that voice behind him.

He turned savagely. "I thought I told you—"

"Very well. I'll go. You needn't glare at me so. Besides, if one of those big shells should strike us, the cabin would be no safer than the deck. I'll go forward and talk to San Thoy, who can't be more disagreeable."

Kantar removed the clip of explosive shells and inserted one of solid shot. He would try to let some water into these ships. That would slow them up. He took aim, and held his finger on the firing button. The weapon poured forth a steady stream of projectiles. When the clip was empty, he inserted another, and riddled the other ship below the water line. The enemy shells were screaming closer, and in larger numbers. Only one shell, he knew, properly placed, would completely destroy their little craft.

Suddenly he heard their own forward mattork go into action. Looking back over the low roof of the cabin, he saw that San Thoy was still steering. Then he knew that Narine was operating that mattork. Moreover, she was using explosive shells, and had scored several hits.

Having punctured both ships below their water lines, Kantar decided to try to cripple their masts. Accordingly he reloaded, this time with explosive shells. As he bent to his task, his hands worked almost mechanically. He was thinking, not of their danger, not even of Grandon and Vernia. Strange to say, the thought that dominated his mind at that moment was, that Narine was very beautiful.

He was suddenly recalled to stark reality as a solid projectile struck their own mast, carrying it overboard, and leaving them at the mercy of their pursuers.

CHAPTER XV

BEASTS OF THE ANTARCTIC

ALTHOUGH HE PLAINLY SAW THE IBBIT warrior left to slay him by the savage chieftain who had abducted Vernia, Grandon continued to drop swiftly from balcony to balcony as if contemptuous of his furry enemy. As his feet struck the lowest balcony, the long lance with its corkscrew head was thrust at him, and he now saw its purpose and how deadly it could be, for the warrior pulled a small lever like a trigger, as he thrust, and the head whirled so rapidly that its outlines blurred.

He leaped lightly aside just in time to avoid that whirling deadly point. Then before the Ibbit could draw it back for a second thrust, he whipped out his scarbo, and extending the point, dived straight over the railing at his enemy.

Taken completely by surprize at this daring and desperate move of the Earth-man, the furry fighter tried to dodge the swiftly descending point. But he moved too late. With the full weight of Grandon behind it, the blade of the scarbo was driven through his body up to the hilt, and he lunged out of the saddle.

Grandon and the corpse of his would-be slayer struck the ground together. Withdrawing his scarbo, the Earth-man sprang to his feet. To his consternation, he saw that the blade had been snapped off about ten inches from the hilt. Then he noticed that his fallen foe wore a scarbo, and quickly appropriated it. He also took his huge cloak and hood of zandar fur, his long fur boots and gauntlets, and his lance.

By this time Heg, Rogo of the Ibbits, and his warriors, were half-way to the city gate. Grandon knew that the only possible way to catch them would be for him to mount and ride the strange and formidable looking beast whose rider he had just slain. The creature was evidently well trained; for despite the fight which had brought it a change of masters, it kept its place beneath the balcony, complacently chewing its cud.

On Earth, Grandon had been accounted a good rider, but here were beast and equipment both of which were new to him. The savage-looking mount was saddled, but wore neither bridle nor halter. He had no idea how it could be guided, started, or stopped, but there was nothing for him except to climb into the saddle and investigate: This he did.

"Go ahead," he said, in patoa. Without moving, the beast continued its contented cud-chewing. Instinctively, he dug his heels into its sides as if he had worn spurs. So suddenly that he was almost unseated, the zandar sprang forward. But it was going in the wrong direction. How to turn it was the next problem. He tried slapping its neck, first on one side, then on the other, without effect. Then he tried pressing alternately with the right and left knees with no result. Baffled, he grasped the creature's mane, determined to spring from the saddle and follow the Ibbits on foot. Instantly the beast slowed down and stopped.

If he could only find out how to turn the creature! Once more he dug his heels into its sides and the animal sprang forward. He heard someone shout, and turned to see who it was. A group of Huitsenni had discovered the dead Ibbit beneath the balcony. But when he turned, he advanced his right foot and drew back his left. Instantly the zandar whirled to the left. Quickly he returned his feet to the normal position, whereupon the beast settled down to a straight course. He advanced his left foot and drew back his right, and the zandar turned to the right. Now able to guide his strange mount, he set off in swift pursuit of the Ibbits.

The hoofs of his speeding zandar beat a rumbling tattoo on the planking of the broad street, and he dug his heels into its sides to urge it to greater efforts. The Ibbits, he observed, had been stopped at the city gate. The mojak of the guard was evidently suspicious because of their abrupt departure.

Grandon wondered if the body of Yin Yin had been discovered. Probably not, he thought, as the room in which he had been slain was segregated from the others; and of those who had witnessed his death, there had been none left alive to carry the news. It would be discovered eventually, of course. But in the meantime, the Ibbits might be well away from the city.

He was about a quarter of a mile from the party of Ibbits he was striving to catch when he saw the gates thrown open. A moment later, the boom of a mattork sounded from the direction of the palace, and a shell screamed over his head. Then he knew that the body of Yin Yin had been discovered. The firing of the mattork was evidently a signal to the mojak of the guard, who threw a party of his warriors in front of the Ibbits and tried to close the gates.

Instantly, the Ibbits couched their long lances, and charged. There was a popping of tork fire from the thin line of guards, but they were swept away like straw before a gale. Some were trampled underfoot, some were gored by the horns of the charging beasts, and the rest impaled and swung off their feet on the long lances, to be thrown over the head of the first-line riders and trampled beneath the hoofs of the cavalcade that followed.

In his anxiety to catch that charging column, Grandon dug his heels into the ribs of his mount with all his might. But the beast, evidently traveling at its utmost speed already, did not respond in any way except to grunt angrily.

He arrived at the gate about a hundred yards behind the last Ibbit in the column, in a hail of mattork shells from the palace. A single man barred his way— the mojak. Evidently all the others had been slain.

Elevating the muzzle of his tork, the officer sent a bullet uncomfortably close to Grandon's ear. Couching his lance, he pulled back the lever, and the corkscrew head began revolving with terrific speed. It struck the mojak in the middle, and instantly drilled through him, up to the knob. Not knowing how to release his weapon from the body, Grandon dropped it, and stooping from the saddle, caught up another which was lying beside a dead Ibbit. With this he experimented as he hurried forward to join the furry savages. He found that when the lever was pulled back, the head revolved clockwise, literally screwing itself into its victim. When the lever was perpendicular to the shaft, it stopped, but when it was pushed forward, the head immediately revolved in a counter-clockwise direction, thus swiftly unscrewing itself from anything in which it might be imbedded. This explained how the Ibbits were able to impale their victims and then hurl them over their heads without losing their lances.

The last faint glow from the city lights was disappearing as Grandon caught up with the rear guard of the Ibbits. Now, at intervals of about fifty feet in the column, riders lighted torches. Muffled up as he was, however, with the hood throwing his

features into shadow, Grandon did not fear recognition unless the sound of his voice or his accent should make someone
suspicious. Suddenly a rider beside him turned and put him
to the test: "Did you slay the strange warrior?" he asked.

Grandon pretended to be seized with a fit of coughing. Then,
in the rasping tones of a man whose vocal cords have not
yet recovered from such an attack, he replied: "I ran him
through the heart. He will trouble us no more."

"Good!" exclaimed the rider, evidently unsuspicious. "His
Majesty was worried about that fellow. He feared that he
would find a way to follow, and come upon him by
stealth. You will be well rewarded."

Grandon smiled to himself, and made no further comment.
Far up near the front of the column he saw a rider carrying a
fur-covered bundle which he believed to be Vernia. But he
did not deem it advisable to ride too near the Rogo just yet.
There might be questions to answer, and he felt sure that,
sooner or later, his voice would betray him unless he could
manage to keep from speaking.

Presently they entered a belt of tall trees, primitive conifers,
where the trail began to slant sharply upward. Here the beasts
slowed down to a walk, though they did not seem greatly in-
convenienced by the steepness of the ascent.

As they climbed higher and higher, the air kept growing
colder, until Grandon, who had been uncomfortably warm in
his furs when on the low ground, was now thankful for them.
Soon he noticed that the ground was powdered with a white
substance. It was snow, the first he had seen on Venus. Also,
he began to be aware of furtive, slinking forms flitting among
the tree trunks, trotting beside the cavalcade. Their eyes
glowed weirdly green in the torchlight, but it was some time
before he could make out what they were. Then one, bolder
than the rest, approached to within fifty feet of the riders,
and he got a good look at it. It was a white awoo. Some
time later he caught sight of a white marmelot, tearing at

the carcass of some beast it had slain. And he began to wonder if all creatures, here in the Zorovian antarctic, were white.

The snow grew deeper as they advanced, and the trees more stunted. Presently they crossed a narrow ridge and filed out onto level ground—a snow-covered plateau, its bleak surface swept by a bitterly cold wind laden with powdered ice particles that pricked the skin like needles. Here, despite the deep snow, the zandars made good progress. This was their natural habitat, and they were equipped for it. Their broad, three-toed feet kept them from sinking deeply, and with their thick, silky coats, Grandon judged that they were more comfortable than in the lower, warmer country.

All through the night, the shaggy beasts kept up their tireless pace. But when morning dawned, the calvalcade halted in a little clump of stunted trees that afforded some protection from the wind, for rest and refreshment.

The zandars, with their saddles still on them, were turned loose to shift for themselves. Grandon saw them eagerly devouring a species of purple moss that grew on top of the snow and sent long, thread-like roots to the soil, far below. They also browsed on such aromatic shoots as they were able to reach on the lower branches of the trees.

Soon the Ibbits had a fire crackling. Then two huge pots were set upon it and snow was shoveled into them to melt. As soon as sufficient water was thus obtained, strips of frozen meat were dropped into the larger of the two pots, and chopped kova roots into the smaller. Vernia was placed near the fire. The rogo sat near her, endeavoring to engage her in conversation, but without success. On the other side of the fire the warriors sprawled in a semicircle, chatting, laughing, and eagerly watching the operations of two of their number who were acting as cooks.

With the coming of the dawn, Grandon had been especially careful to keep his hood pulled forward, so that his features would not be noticed. Now, as he sat among the warriors, he kept his head bowed as an additional precaution.

Presently the two cooks went among the men, serving the stewed meat and steaming bowls of kova. Grandon found the meat tough and rather tasteless, but welcome, nevertheless, after his long ride. The kova was well brewed, and refreshing.

After they had eaten and drunk, the warriors stretched out in the snow to sleep. Grandon, perforce, followed their example for fear of becoming conspicuous, but managed to turn his head so that he could watch Vernia and the Rogo. The chieftain, after unsuccessfully urging his fair prisoner to get some rest, lay down himself. As soon as it appeared that he was asleep, Grandon drew back his hood, then raised one arm to attract the attention of Vernia, who sat staring moodily into the fire. Her eyes attracted by the motion of the arm, she glanced toward him, then smothered an exclamation of surprise and pleasure. Instantly he whipped the hood back over his face and lowered his arm.

Now, seeing that she was covertly watching him, he began slowly rolling away from the others, and motioned to her to edge away from beside the fire at the same time. He hoped that if they could get away from the sleepers with sufficient stealth they could catch two of the grazing zandars, and put a considerable distance between themselves and the Ibbits before the ruse would be discovered.

But his plans were suddenly upset by an agonized bellowing from one of the zandars, followed by a tremendous hissing sound which brought every warrior to his feet. Grandon sprang erect with the others, and saw a monster with a gigantic, lizard-like body to which was attached a scaly serpentine neck and head, biting immense mouthfuls of flesh from the zandar it had just struck down, and which it was holding beneath one huge front claw. Save for its color—for its body was completely covered by gleaming white scales—it might have a silticum, one of those dangerous lizards he had first encountered in the fern forests of Reabon.

"A posilticum! A posilticum!" shouted the warriors. Catching up their spiral-pointed spears, they charged the monster.

The word "po" means "snow" in patoa, so Grandon quickly recognized the import of the name, which might be translated "snow lizard," or "snow dragon."

Like the others, Grandon caught up his lance, and was about to join them in their attack on the monster, when another idea suddenly came to him. He noticed that the Rogo of the Ibbits, although he had sprung to his feet, had not moved from his place beside Vernia. The chieftain noticed his hesitation at the same time, and cried: "What ! Does a warrior of mine fear a posilticum? Go at once with the others, or stay to receive your Rogo's blade."

Nothing could have suited Grandon better. Flinging down his lance, he whipped out his scarbo and leaped across the dying embers of the fire. The chieftain was evidently a good scarboman as Ibbits go, for it appeared that he thought to make short work of Grandon as he struck out with his own blade. It was a cut for the head, which the Earth-man parried. Countering with the same stroke, he found the blade of the Rogo there to meet his. Leaping back to avoid a horizontal blow at the neck, he suddenly changed from the well-established Zorovian practice of using the scarbo as a cutting weapons, and presented his point, lunging for the breast of the barbarian.

Heg was not prepared for this innovation. Nor had he time to come on guard after the terrific slash he had directed at Grandon's neck. The Earth-man's blade tore through his heart, and he toppled backward, dead.

A quick glance around showed Grandon that his duel with the furry Rogo had not been observed by the others, all of whom were skipping about the posilticum, lunging at it with their spiral lances, and leaping back to avoid the darting of its huge and terrible head. The noise they made, the hissing of the posilticum, the bellowing of frightened zandars, and the shouts of the Ibbits, had drowned all sound of the clashing scarbos.

"Come," said Grandon, cleaning and sheathing his blade and catching up his lance. "Now is our chance."

Hand in hand, he and Vernia ran to where a group of frightened zandars cowered together as if for mutual protection. He helped her to mount one of the shaggy beasts, and gave her swift instructions for riding it. Then he leaped to the back of another, and they were off.

As soon as they left the shelter of the trees, the cold wind and stinging snow particles buffeted them unmercifully. They had not been gone more than a few minutes when a terrific blizzard swept down on them. Grandon laid their course in the direction he judged to be northwest, intending to circle Huitsen and make for the shore of the Azpok. He believed that a half-day's ride would take them to the edge of the plateau, and that by descending for a few miles they could find relief from the cold and snow.

But they rode more than a half-day without seeing any sign of the slope for which they were searching. Then a steep cliff, the summit of which was invisible in the whirling cloud of snowflakes, suddenly loomed ahead. They rode up to its base, and, skirting it for some distance, came at length to a dark opening in the rock, half closed by a snow drift. By this time, the zandars, which had traveled nearly all night and half the day with only an hour's rest, began to balk, and Grandon judged that it was best to permit them to rest, and at the same time take advantage of this natural shelter.

He accordingly dismounted, and leaving Vernia to watch the two beasts, cut a path through the snow into the cave with the aid of the whirling spiral point of his lance. Then, lighting his small flamemaker, and keeping the lance in readiness for an attack by a possible unseen enemy, he explored the place. He found himself in a room about twenty feet wide and fifty feet

long, evidently chiseled from the rock by some prehistoric
race, as it had the appearance of having been untenanted for
ages. Mixed with the dust and litter of the ages, which strewed
the floor, were a few partly calcined bones and some fragments
of pottery, which showed that the primitives who had once
lived here were acquainted with the use of fire.

Having satisfied himself that the place was untenanted, Grandon went back for Vernia and the two beasts. The zandars
seemed glad for this shelter from the storm, and lay down
immediately, to rest and chew their cuds.

Gathering some bits of dried wood from the debris on the
floor, Grandon made a small cooking fire near the entrance.
As he had no large pots, he grilled some of the frozen meat
from the saddlebags over the coals, and they made kova in the
two copper drinking bowls which were part of the equipment
in the saddlebags of the Ibbits.

Having eaten and drunk, they snuggled themselves in their
furs, and it was not long before both, weary with the long
ordeal through which they had passed, were asleep.

Vernia was the first to waken. She made two discoveries
in rapid succession—first that a new day had dawned, and
second that their mounts were not in the cave.

"Bob!" she cried. "The zandars are gone!"

He sat up and yawned. "Yes dear, Oh, the zandars.
They've probably gone out to get their breakfast. I'll go and
round them up."

"I'll help you."

"No, you'd better stay here where it's safe and warm."

"But I'll be all right, Bob. I have my furs."

Together they went outside, after Grandon did a little pre-
liminary shoveling with his lance. The storm had passed,
succeeded by a calm, bitter cold that was even more penetrating than the wind of the day before.

"No tracks," said Grandon. "They must have left before the
blizzard was over. Looks as if we're in for it."

"Oh, Bob, what will we do?"

"Nothing to do but strike out on foot, if we can't find them. But we may as well have a look around first. You wait here, and I'll follow the cliff toward the south for a little way. I noticed quite a bit of purple moss growing there yesterday, and those beasts may have remembered, and gone back for it."

"Just in case they went the other way, I'll take a look in that direction," said Vernia.

"Better wait here. It will be safer."

"I don't see why. I won't go far, and I feel the need of a tramp before breakfast. Besides, the beasts may have gone toward the north, in which case we will save time by searching in both directions at once. Go ahead, and don't worry about me."

"Well, if you must. But don't go far, and don't be long."

She watched him for a moment as he strode off along the cliff, then turned and started in the opposite direction. She had gone only a short distance when her attention was attracted by what looked like the prickly segment of a species of Zorovian cactus projecting from behind a bend in the wall.

Puzzled, she walked forward to investigate, but scarcely had she rounded the bend, ere an immense white monster with eight bristly white legs ending in green claws, and a long, jointed tail, darted out and seized her with a pair of huge green chelae, much like the pincers of a lobster. It was one of these that she had mistaken for a segment of cactus. Running swiftly backward, it carried her into a large cave.

Through the center of the cave, from side to side, was stretched an immense web of rope-thick strands, coated with a gleaming, sticky-looking substance. And suspended in one corner of this hung one of the zandars. Beside the helpless beast was a ball about ten feet in diameter, woven of the same gleaming strands. The other zandar hung in a similar mesh-work, near the center of the web.

So suddenly had it happened that Vernia had time to utter but one smothered scream of terror as she was dragged into the cave. Nor could she make any move to defend herself. The huge chelae held her like the jaws of a vise, their coarse, spiny hairs piercing her flesh through the heavy cloak she wore.

Holding her thus, the monster stopped, and standing on four legs, used the other four to draw a sticky white cord from beneath its abdomen and swiftly weave it around her, until she was scarcely able to move a finger. Then it ran up the web to the corner where zandar hung beside the white ball, and fastened her next to the helpless beast.

Having shaken the web several times to make sure that she was fastened securely, the gigantic strid, or spinner-scorpion, for such she recognized it to be, returned to the zandar near the center, and settled down over it to feed. As the wretched beast made no outcry, it was evident that it had either been paralyzed by the terrible telson, the poisonous sting at the end of the jointed tail, or slain by the immense chelae.

For some time, Vernia watched the monster at its bloody feast. Then her attention was attracted by a rustling sound quite near her. She turned, and saw that it came from the quite near her. She turned, and saw that it came from the white ball beside which she was suspended. Something, many

Presently there was a sound as of tearing fabric. A hole appeared in the ball, and out of it came a pair of wiggling, hairy chelae, small replicas of those of the mother scorpion. They were followed by an armored head in which were set three pairs of glowing eyes, blinking dully out at the world for the first time. It was then that Vernia realized what was in store for her. The monster had suspended both her and the zandar beside its cocoon as food for her young when they should break through the shell.

Even as this horrible realization came to her, the first young strid forced its way through the opening, and came ambling across the web toward her on its eight hairy legs.

C H A P T E R XVI

Zinlo Of Olba

WITH ITS MAST SHOT AWAY, THE LITTLE sailboat in which rode Kantar the Gunner, Narine of Tyrhana, and San Thoy of Huitsen, would not respond to the rudder, but came about and drifted broadside to the waves, rocking precariously while mattork shells exploded all around it. The two pursuing pirate ships now bore down on the helpless boat.

Despite the increased difficulty of aiming his weapon, occasioned by the erratic plunging of the little craft, the skilful gunner succeeded in shattering a few spars and damaging the rigging of one of their pursuers with his explosive bullets. But as the two ships drew closer, he ceased firing, knowing that in surrender now lay their only hope of life. Abandoning his weapon, he hurried forward, where he found Narine still endeavoring to manage the other mattork.

"Stop shooting," he said, "or the pirates will blow us to pieces. They are bound to hit us when they get a little closer."

"I hope they do," she replied as she fired another shot, which, on account of the rocking of the boat, went wide of the mark. "To me death is preferable to falling again into their hands."

As if in answer to her wish, a shell struck them aft, the next moment, completely demolishing the stern. Kantar and Narine were both hurled against the cabin by the force of the concussion, and San Thoy shot from his steersman's seat to a point on the deck quite near them. The hold filled almost instantly, and the boat plunged beneath the waves.

As they went down, Kantar seized Narine's wrist. A moment later they came up, struggling and sputtering in the water.

"Let me go," she demanded, as soon as she could get her breath. "I can take care of myself."

The gunner relinquished her wrist, and grinning maliciously, said: "Well, you had your wish. I hope you are enjoying the consequences."

Without replying, she turned and swam for a bit of wreckage larger than the others that bobbed around them. It had once been part of the after deck. Kantar looked around for San Thoy, and seeing him clinging to a heavy beam which could easily support him in the water, he leisurely followed Narine. The pirate ship ceased firing, and one of them was now only three hundred yards distant.

Swimming up beside the girl's bit of wreckage, Kantar rested an arm upon it.

"May I share this luxurious float with you?" he asked, smiling.

"If you will try to be agreeable," she answered. "But one more word of sarcasm, and I'll—"

"You'll what?"

"Duck you."

"Try it."

She did, forcing his head, unresisting, under water. She held it there until she considered that his punishment had been sufficient, then removed her hand. But he didn't come up. Instead, his face remained under water, and he floated limply there beside the wreckage. She pulled his hair, but got no response. Alarmed, she moved closer, and lifted his head from the water.

The gunner, who had been shamming, peered at her beneath lowered lids—saw the consternation in her pretty face—saw her red lips so close to his. A maddening desire from them overcame him.

"Kantar!" she cried. "Oh, what have I done?"

Suddenly he swept her to him, crushed her lips to his.

She trembled there in his embrace for a moment, then broke from him, her face scarlet.

"You would dare!" she exclaimed. "Oh, you beast! You are worse than the Huitsenni, none of whom has ventured to so affront me."

"Narine," he pleaded, "I love you. I must tell you this before I go to my death at the hands of those yellow pirates, for they will surely slay me after what I have done. Your lips drew me—twin lodestones I could not resist. If you cannot return my love, can you at least forgive me?"

Her look softened. "The pirates have lowered a boat," she said, "so I must put maidenly modesty aside and answer you briefly and truthfully. I do love you, my brave gunner. I have loved you from the moment I first saw you, there in the cabin of the little fishing boat. But even had I hope of life and freedom, I could never marry you."

"There is another man?"

"Yes. My father. He would never consent."

"Perhaps he could be brought to reason."

"Impossible. You see my older sister disappointed him in his plans for a matrimonial alliance, and fell in love with him, but he will not be turned again from his purpose. Her disappointed lover has agreed to solace himself with me. My father will not give in so easily a second time.

"But all this talk is futile. We are once more in the power of the Huitsenni, and only they may decide our fate. Here is the boat. Farewell, my gunner, and may Thorth guide and keep you."

"I'll never give you up," he cried.

Yellow hands seized them, dragged them into the boat. Then Kantar suddenly saw what he had no opportunity to see before. When the boat had gone down, Narine's improvised cloak had floated from her. Later, all but her head, arms, and shoulders had been under water. But now he observed that she wore scarlet of royalty, and on the golden breast shields he saw the insignia of an imperial princess of Tyrhana. All the hopes which her words had aroused died in his heart. For Kantar was but a common soldier. His father had been an officer in the Uxponian army, but without even the purple of nobility.

Narine saw the despair in his eyes, and guessed his thoughts. She smiled a little wistful smile.

"I understand now," said the gunner. Then he resolutely turned his head away, and meekly permitted his captors to bind his wrists. A moment later, San Thoy also was dragged out of the water.

Swiftly the rowers propelled the boat back to the ship. The prisoners were hoisted aboard. Narine was hurried away by the mojak of the vessel. And with kicks and cuffs, Kantar and San Thoy, bound hand and foot, were thrown into an evil-smelling room in the hold, quite similar to the one in which they had been confined with Grandon when first taken to Huitsen. Immediately Kantar set about trying to loose the bonds of his companion.

But his tedious labors were suddenly interrupted by an explosion which tore a hole in the planking above their heads.

There followed the rapid booming of mattorks, the screaming of projectiles, and the almost continuous bursting of shells.

"Our captors must have found new victims," said Kantar, springing to his feet.

"Judging by the number of shells which are striking this ship, I would say that they are more likely to become the victims," replied San Thoy, also getting to his feet.

Both men hopped to the side of the boat—they could not walk because of their bound feet—and peered through the loopholes.

"Bones of Thorth!" exclaimed San Thoy. "There are ships floating in the air!"

Looking out, Kantar saw a fleet of aerial battleships. They were shaped like duck-boats, surmounted by heavy transparent turrets mounting heavy mattorks, and flew without wings, rudders or propellers.

"They are Olban airships," he said. "I once saw a fleet of them in Reabon."

"Never before have I seen or heard of such marvellous craft above the Azpok," said San Thoy.

"It's strange that they should be here. I wonder— ah! I have it. Zinlo, Torrogo of Olva, is fiancé of Loralie, the Torrogina of Tyrhana. Naturally he would, on being advised of the disappearance of her younger sister, assist in the search for her. And just as naturally, he would attack the ships of the Huitsenni, who are enemies to all Zorovia, wherever he should find them."

For several minutes the bombardment became more intense, and Kantar was much concerned for Narine's safety. Then a huge shadow darkened the waters before them, the bombardment ceased, and there was the noise of grappling hooks scraping across the splintered decks. These sounds were succeeded by the tramping of many feet above them, the clashing of arms intermingled with the spitting of tork fire, and a medley of shouts, groans, and shrieks.

"The Olbans have boarded us," said Kantar. "I trust they arrive in time to save Narine."

The fighting was soon over. And presently the gunner heard the tramp of warriors, evidently searching the ship, passing their door. "Ho, Olbans," he called, "open the door."

"Who is it?" a voice asked, cautiously.

"A warrior of Reabon and a fellow prisoner," he replied.

The door was unbolted and flung open. Three Olban warriors, with the muzzles of their torks elevated, peered in, while a fourth flashed a light about the room. Seeing the two bound men, they entered and quickly released them.

"Have they found the princess?" Kantar inquired, rubbing his numbed wrists. "Is she safe?"

"What princess?" asked the soldier who had removed his bonds. "We know naught of a princess."

"Why, Narine, Torrogini of Tyrhana," replied the gunner. "She was captured and brought aboard with us."

"Ha! It is as His Majesty suspected," cried another soldier. "From a distance we saw them sink a small boat, and later lower a boat to bring away three people from the wreckage. Yet their mojak has stoutly denied that he had prisoners aboard. Come. The Torrogo must hear of this at once."

With the four Olbans, they hurried to the deck. A group of Huitsenni prisoners huddled, weaponless, in the stern, under the watchful eyes of several guards. Warriors were heaving the bodies of the slain overboard, and Olban surgeons were tending the wounded, both friend and foe. Attached to the side of the vessel by hooks and chains was an immense aerial battleship with twelve gun turrets. A set of collapsible aluminum stairs led from an open door in one of these turrets to the deck of the ship. On the opposite side, another aerial battleship was similarly fastened. A fleet of a dozen more airships floated overhead, and Kantar saw that the other pirate ship had also been boarded by the crews of two aerial battleships, and its men subdued.

They hurried forward. On the foredeck stood a handsome young man of about the gunner's own age, whom Kantar instantly recognized as Zinlo, Torrogo of Olba. He was clad in scarlet apparel, gold-trimmed and glittering with precious stones. On his feet were sandals of soft frella hide, and his scarlet, turban-shaped headpiece was decked with gold fringe and set with a huge ruby that blazed above the center of his forehead. Beside him stood an equally youthful soldier, whose insignia proclaimed him Romojak of the Aerial Navies of Olba.

On his knees before the young Torrogo was the mojak of the vessel. As Kantar came up with the others he was saying: "I swear to you, Majesty, by the beard and body of Thorth, by all I hold sacred, that I have no prisoners, white or yellow, on board."

"So. You persist in your falsehood." Zinlo frowned at the yellow man who groveled before him. Then his eyes fell on Kantar and San Thoy.

"Whom have we here?" he asked one of the warriors who had released them.

The mojak looked around, and seeing who stood behind him, turned a pale, sickly yellow.

"They are two prisoners we found in a room below the deck, Your Majesty," replied the warrior.

Kantar made obeisance, with right hand extended palm downward.

"I am Kantar the Gunner, of Reabon, Your Majesty," he said, "and my companion is San Thoy, a former mojak in the navy of Huitsen. If you don't mind, I would prefer to tell you our story after Her Imperial Highness has been found."

"Her Imperial Highness?"

"I refer, Your Majesty, to Narine, Torrogini of Tyrhana."

"Ha!" Zinlo suddenly whipped out his scarbo and presented its point to the breast of the frightened mojak. "Now, you yellow hahoe, we have caught you lying. Either you will tell us, this instant, where the Princess is concealed, or I will slay you, and if need be, tear this ship apart to find her."

"Mercy, Majesty! Have mercy!" quavered the mojak. "I will show you."

Rising, and backing away from the royal presence, he stooped and seized a ring in the deck, Pulling this, he lifted a trap door from which a short ladder led down into a small cabin. Lying on the sleeping shelf of the cabin was Narine, gagged, and bound hand and foot.

Disdaining the ladder, Kantar dropped into the cabin, closely followed by the young Torrogo. Together they quickly unbound the princess and removed her gag. She was limp, and apparently lifeless.

"Narine! Narine!" For the moment Kantar, who knelt beside the sleeping shelf, forgot the presence of Zinlo of Olba—forgot that the girl before him was an imperial princess.

Narine opened her eyes and saw Kantar bending over her. But Zinlo she did not see. Her right arm went around the gunner's neck—her hand carressed his sandy hair. "I'm just a little faint, my gunner. That gag made breathing difficult. I could not have lasted much longer."

He caught up her left hand, lying limply beside her, and covered it with kisses. "I'm glad, so glad, we came in time."

"My lips, Gunner. Have they lost their allure so quickly?" She drew his face down to hers.

Zinlo raised a quizzical eyebrow. Then, with a fierce gesture, he waved off the gaping warriors who were peering down at them.

"I heard explosions—men fighting on the decks. Tell me what happened," said Narine, a moment later.

"His Imperial Majesty, Zinlo of Olba, rescued us," replied Kantar, suddenly remembering the presence of the Torrogo, and blushing furiously in consequence.

"What!" Narine sat up quickly, then seeing Zinlo, turned to face him, her shapely legs dangling from the sleeping shelf.

"Your Majesty!" she cried in consternation. "I did not know you were here."

She rose and made the customary obeisance.

"I surmised as much, Your Highness," smiled Zinlo. Then he took her extended hand, and kneeling, raised it to his lips. "Shall we adjourn to more comfortable quarters?"

"Let's. I've always wanted to ride in one of your Olban airships. What of my father and sister?"

"Both well, but almost frantic with worry on account of you."

When they reached the deck, the young romojak, who had been standing beside Zinlo when Kantar first saw him, came up and saluted.

"What is it, Lotar?" asked Zinlo.

"We have disposed of all prisoners in accordance with Your Majesty's commands," replied the romojak. "There remains, however, the yellow man we found imprisoned with this warrior of Reabon."

"Take him aboard the flagship," said Zinlo, "and see that he has every comfort."

Lotar saluted and withdrew. Then the three climbed the aluminum stairs, and after passing through a narrow hallway, entered the luxurious saloon of Zinlo's flagship. The young Torrogo placed cushioned chairs for both of them, and summoned a slave. "Bring us kova," he commanded.

He drew up a chair and sat down. Then he noticed that Kantar, conforming to the usages of the court, had not seated himself because he was in the presence of royalty. "Sit, Gunner," he said. "We will have no formality here."

This was a command, and Kantar, whose feeling of embarrassment had only slightly lessened since the incident in the cabin, took the chair which had been placed for him.

The slave bustled in with kova, and Zinlo himself served his guests in tiny bowls of gold lined with mother of pearl.

"Now," he said, "as soon as my Romojak comes aboard, we'll fly to the flagship of Ad of Tyrhana. But in the meantime, Your Highness, suppose you tell me what you have been doing these many days."

"My father's flagship!" exclaimed Narine. "Where is he?"

"Only a little way from here," replied Zinlo, "and Loralie is with him. But let's hear that story."

Swiftly, Narine sketched for him the story of her adventures —the storm, her capture by the Huitsenni, her sale to Heg and rescue by Kantar, and their escape with the aid of San Thoy.

Zinlo frowned. "These yellow pirates must be wiped out," he said, "and there is no better time than now to do it. But what of my friend Grandon and his beautiful bride?" he asked Kantar. "Do you think they were both carried off by the white-furred barbarians?"

"I think it probable," replied Kantar, "that her Majesty was carried off by Heg. It is possible that the Ibbits also took Grandon prisoner, but I think it more probable that he found some way to follow the savages, in an effort to rescue his bride."

"I'll send a squadron after them," said Zinlo. "As I judge from what Her Highness just told me that the capital of the furry Rogo is five days journey from Huitsen, my swift air-ships can easily overtake them before they reach their destination."

At this moment, Lotar came in and saluted.

"To the flagship of Ad of Tyrhana," commanded Zinlo. "Signal the fleet to attend us. You have placed the prize crews aboard the two pirate vessels?"

"Yes, Majesty." He saluted and withdrew.

A moment later the ship rose smoothly and swiftly to a height of about two thousand feet, then shot away toward the west at a tremendous speed. Kantar, who had never ridden in one of these craft before, but had heard that the swiftest ones were capable of traveling at the speed with which the planet revolved on its axis at the equator—approximately a thousand miles an hour—nevertheless marveled at the speed with which the ocean appeared to move beneath them as he watched through one of the side windows. Sailing on the waves of the Azpok, he now saw six large battle fleets, all within a few miles of the spot where their little craft had been sunk by the Huitsenni.

The airship reached a point over the flagship of one of these fleets and swiftly descended.

Narine placed a hand on Zinlo's arm. "You won't tell my father?" she asked.

"About what?" Zinlo appeared puzzled.

She looked tenderly at Kantar. "About us. We know it is hopeless, our love, and have agreed to—to—"

"Try to forget," suggested Zinlo.

"You're so helpful, my brother to be. But there in the cabin, for the moment, love mastered us."

"I understand, perfectly," said the young Torrogo.

"Of course. You and Loralie—"

"Exactly."

"But my father will not be moved from his purpose again. I know him well enough for that."

"Oh, I don't know. What has been done before can be done again. Perhaps I can do something."

"You are so kind. Now I know why Loralie just can't help loving you. But for the present at least, you will say nothing?"

"In that cabin, I was deaf, dumb, and blind, as were my warriors who happened to be peering down at us. But here we are at the flagship."

Kantar heard the clank of chains and the thud of grappling irons. Then Zinlo rose, and they followed him down the ladder to the deck of an immense battleship which flew the flag of Ad, Torrogo of Tyrhana.

Just as they reached the deck, the gunner saw two people emerge from one of the cabins—a tall, straight, athletic-appearing man about forty years of age, with a square-cut, jet-black beard, and a girl who closely resembled Narine, though she appeared a trifle more mature. Both wore the scarlet of royalty, and Kantar knew that they must be Ad of Tyrhana and his daughter, Loralie.

Narine ran into the open arms of her father, then embraced her sister. All three shed tears of joy, and Kantar, whose own eyes were overflowing, saw that Zinlo was in like case.

The gunner was presented, and all were ushered into Ad's sumptuous cabin, where the customary kova was served.

After Narine had related the story of her adventures, Kantar was pressed to tell his, and those of Grandon and Vernia with which he was acquainted.

When the gunner had finished, Ad echoed the previously expressed sentiment of Zinlo. "We must wipe out the Huitsenni," he declared. "But first we must try to rescue their Majesties of Reabon."

"I'm going to send a squadron after the Ibbits," said Zinlo.

"But suppose Grandon and his bride are still in Huitsen."

"I believe we can ascertain whether or not they are there," said Kantar.

"How?" asked Ad.

"The Chispoks. There must be some members among the pirates you have captured. Land some of them near the city under cover of darkness. Let them investigate, and report back to you."

"A splendid idea," said Zinlo. "And I would suggest a further plan. Suppose we form an alliance with the Chispoks, overthrow the present regime, if indeed they have not done so already, and put them in power. That would be better than indiscriminately wiping out the entire yellow race, all of whom are certainly not responsible for the piratical outrages of Yin Yin's men. The port of Huitsen could then be opened for peaceful trade with all Zorovia, and if the Huitsenni should ever again develop piratical leanings, we would know how to stop them."

"I'm sure the alliance can be arranged, Your Majesty," said Kantar. "Suppose we send for San Thoy."

Zinlo called a servant. "Tell my romojak to bring San Thoy, the yellow man, here," he directed.

In a few moments Lotar came in, accompanied by San Thoy. Kantar presented the former mojak of the navy of Huitsen to the assemblage. Then Zinlo addressed Lotar. Briefly he told him why they suspected that Grandon and Vernia might be traveling southward with a party of Ibbits, and gave him his instructions: "Dispatch six ships," he commanded, "with orders to fly high above Huitsen, deep enough in the first cloud stratum so they will not be seen from the city. Then, when they have their bearings, let them spread out, and fly southward until they come to a column of furry white savages riding on three-horned beasts. If Grandon of Terra and his bride are with this party, they must rescue them as best they can, and bring them here at once."

Lotar saluted. "I hasten to carry out Your Majesty's commands," he replied, and hurried out.

As soon as Lotar had gone, San Thoy was quizzed about a possible alliance with the Chispoks. He not only felt positive that he could arrange this, but stated that he had received secret signs from several of the yellow sailors on board the vessel which he had been rescued, which proved to him that they were members of the brotherhood. After a short conference, he was dispatched in one of Zinlo's airships to visit both captured pirate vessels, and cull the Chispoks from among the prisoners.

"What of our allies?" Zinlo asked Ad, after San Thoy had departed. "Shall we let them help in the assault on Huitsen?"

Ad stroked his black beard thoughtfully. "Hum. Let's see. We have two squadrons here, of our own. Lying near by are two from Adonijar, and a little farther away, two from Reabon."

"In addition to their battleships, the Reabonians have two score transports, and as many munition ships, with a large army and munitions and equipment for a land offensive," said Zinlo.

"I was thinking of that," said Ad. "How or where could they land their army?"

"The Chispoks know a secret way," said Kantar. "San Thoy or one of his fellows could guide them."

"Splendid. We can now plan a united offensive. The Reabonians will disembark at night, and guided by the Chispoks, will march on Huitsen, prepared for an offensive tomorrow at an hour we shall set. You, Zinlo, will mass your aerial battleships above the city to join in the attack at the same time, and to convey signals from one force to another. Meanwhile, the battleships of Tyrhana, Adonijar, and Reabon must find some way to get through the secret entrance."

"I've thought of a plan for that, also, Your Majesty," said Kantar.

"Good. Let me hear it, my boy."

And so Kantar related to them a plan he had conceived on the spur of the moment, whereby he believed they could not only get the gates opened for them, but keep them open for the entrance of the battle fleets of the three great nations.

C H A P T E R **XVII**

THE DEATH SENTENCE

SOME TIME AFTER GRANDON AND VERNIA separated at the mouth of the cave to look for their riding-beasts which had disappeared, and which they believed had strayed in search of food, there came faintly to the ears of the the Earth-man a sound that caused him to stop, whirl around, and listen intently. So slight was the sound that he could not quite make it out, yet it had a quality which made him suspicious that Vernia had called him. Though he strained his ears to catch a possible repetition, none was audible.

Alarmed, he retraced his steps as swiftly as possible, but the soft, newly fallen snow retarded his progress considerably. Fuming impatiently at the delay, he floundered past the mouth of the cave in which they had passed the night, and anxiously took up Vernia's trail, shouting her name as he went. But there was no reply.

The tracks led him close to the irregular base of the cliff, and as Grandon stumbled around a bend, he saw the same sight which Vernia had beheld only a short time before, and which had led to her entrapment—a bristly white and green object curving outward from behind a projection, which looked like a segment of Zorovian cactus. Like her, he thought it part of some antarctic plant, and proceeded incautiously toward it. He came to a sudden pause, however, and presented the spiral point of his lance, as the apparent segment resolved itself into one of the chelae of an immense white scorpion, which shot out from behind the projection, and charged swiftly toward him.

Pointing his lance, Grandon pulled back the lever which set the spiral head to whirling. Fearlessly, and without swerving or endeavoring to evade the weapon, the monster sprang at the Earth-man with its immense pincers extended to seize him. Right in the thorax the lance point struck, and bored in up to the knob. Grandon was thrown backward by the impact of that charge, but by diverting the butt of his lance downward and plunging it through the snow until it struck frozen ground beneath, was able to hold the scorpion away from him.

Then still clinging to the shaft with his left hand, he drew his scarbo with his right, and struck at the nearest chela. It was quite tough and horny, and the blade did not bite more than half-way through it. Clenching his teeth, he struck again with all his strength, and this time succeeded in severing it near the middle. Having mastered the art of it, he was able to cut off the other claw at the first joint with two sharp blows.

But no sooner had these menaces been removed than he was threatened with another, even more dangerous. With lightning swiftness, the monster suddenly elevated its long, jointed tail, and stabbed at him with the terrible telson with which the tip was armed.

Avoiding the deadly thrust of the poison sting by leaning sideways, Grandon hacked at the thing with his scarbo. To his surprize, it was quite brittle, and broke off with the first blow.

Although the monster was now unable to injure him except at very close quarters, it was not without resource. It suddenly reached beneath its abdomen with its foremost pair of hairy legs, and drawing therefrom a section of gleaming, sticky web as thick as a rope, it cast the loop about him and dragged him forward. He clung to the lance-shaft with all his might, and succeeded in severing the sticky loop with a stroke of his scarbo. Not so a second loop, however, which it unexpectedly flung around him, breaking his hold on the shaft, as it jerked him toward its ugly gaping mandibles with his right arm bound to his side.

He had previously refrained from using his tork for fear the sound would bring enemies, but in this extremity he elevated the muzzle, depressed the firing-button, and sent a stream of bullets straight into the gaping jaws. With muffled detonations the projectiles exploded in the huge, armored body. A half-dozen of them sufficed to blow the hard-shelled cephalothorax to bits, and reduced the segmented abdomen to a shapeless quivering mass.

Quickly shifting his scarbo to his left hand, Grandon cut himself free of the sticky loop that encumbered him. Then, perceiving the yawning cave mouth, and suspecting that it was here that Vernia had been taken, he rushed inside. Despite their wrappings, he was able to identify the two zandars, one hanging in the center of the huge web, the other at the edge beside a large sperical cocoon. But what was the smaller object beside the cocoon? His heart stood still as he recognized the slender form of Vernia, and saw that a young scorpion, which had evidently just emerged from the cocoon, was crawling toward her.

Although the newly hatched monster was not more than six feet from Vernia, and he could not shoot without endangering her, he knew that there was nothing else to do. Accordingly, he brought his tork to bear on the hairy youngster, and fired. There was a muffled explosion, and the menace was removed. But now he saw another pair of chelae emerging from the coccoon. Again he fired, and the second young scorpion was blown to bits. He watched for a moment, but as no more appeared, decided that the other eggs had not yet hatched, and set about trying to find a way to climb to where Vernia was suspended.

The stickiness of the web made this almost impossible, until he thought to utilize the dust and debris which littered the door. Catching this up in double handfuls, he flung it against the section of the web which he wished to climb, and found, as he hoped, that it prevented the adhesive surface of the strands from clinging to his hands and feet.

Swiftly he climbed up to Vernia, cut the surrounding strands, and as swiftly descended to the floor with his burden. With his knife he quickly slit open the wrappings and found his wife, limp, and apparently lifeless. He opened her great fur cloak, and the sight of several scratches on her white skin engendered the fear that she had been poisoned by the venom of the monster. But when he held his ear to her breast, he was relieved to hear her heart beating.

With a handful of snow taken from the cave mouth, he touched her temples. The cold shock revived her. She looked about wildly for a moment; then, recognizing Grandon, she relaxed contentedly in his arms.

"Are you hurt dear?" he asked.

"Only a few scratches, Bob," she replied. "It was the fright that made me swoon. When I saw that young strid coming toward me, as I hung there helpless, and realized that its purpose was to devour me, I fainted. Let me rest for a little while, and I'll be ready to walk."

"Perhaps you won't need to walk," said Grandon. "One zandar appears to be alive. I'll see if I can cut it down."

Utilizing the dust as he had done before, Grandon succeeded in making a path up the web for himself to where the zandar hung beside the immense cocoon. With his scarbo, he first cut the heavy, rope-like strands above it. Then, as the great bulk of the beast swung downward, he cut the cross strands in succession, and with each cut, the zandar descended a little further. When at last the beast was on the floor, it was still helpless because of the thorough manner in which it had been trussed. But its heaving flanks showed that it was still very much alive, and not a little frightened by the experience it had just gone through. Employing his knife, Grandon quickly cut the strands which held it, and it struggled to its feet, trembling and panting heavily.

"It seems unhurt," said Vernia, who had recovered from her faintness and come over to watch the proceedings.

"Its legs are sound, at any rate," replied Grandon.

The beast followed them docilely enough through the mouth of the cave. Then, after helping Vernia into the saddle, Grandon returned for a moment, to apply his flame-maker to the bottom of the web. It caught fire with a roar, and he plunged out of the cave followed by a billowing cloud of black, oily smoke.

"That will do for the rest of the ugly brood," he said as he came up beside Vernia.

He was about to mount behind her, when he suddenly saw, riding swiftly toward them, a large band of warriors mounted on zandars. They were not Ibbits, as he could see at a glance, but Huitsenni, and had evidently heard his tork fire and come to investigate. Instantly the riders deployed in a wide semi-circle, cutting off all possibility of escape across the snow. As they could not climb the sheer face of the cliff behind them, nor retire into the cave, which was now belching great clouds of acrid smoke, they remained where they were, Vernia still in the saddle, and Grandon beside her.

Had he been alone, Grandon would have resisted desperately, but he knew that if he should use his tork the enemy would retaliate in kind, and Vernia might be injured or slain. A moment more, and he was looking into the mouths of fully a hundred torks leveled at him by a closely packed semicircle of riders. Then the mojak in command ordered a halt, and called out to Grandon: "Surrender, in the name of the Rogo of Huitsen, or we fire."

Seeing that resistance was useless, Grandon unbuckled the belt which contained his weapons, and flung it on the snow in front of him. Then he clasped his hands behind his head in token of surrender.

At the order of the mojak, two men descended and swiftly bound him, hand and foot. Then he was slung across the saddle-bow of one of the riders as if he had been a sack of grain, and the calvalcade rode away. Vernia was not bound, but was permitted to retain her place in the saddle with a guard on each side of her.

Several hours later, it seemed to Grandon that all of Huitsen had turned out to stare at the two prisoners that their riders were bringing in, so dense were the crowds along the streets. Their captors took them straight to the palace, where they were deprived of their Ibbit furs, which were not needed here in the warm lowlands. Then the mojak, quite obviously proud of his success, led them to the throne room, each guarded by two of his warriors.

Up to the time they were ushered into that vast room, Grandon had entertained the hope that one of the Chispoks had succeeded Yin Yin, but his hopes were dashed as he recognized the individual who squatted in the center of the crystal throne. It was the bestial Thid Yet, former Romojak of the Navies of Huitsen. Like his predecessor, he was surrounded by numerous attendants and nobles, and his gross body was loaded with flashing jewels. The porcine monarch grinned toothlessly as they were brought before him.

"It is apparent that our men have persuaded Your Majesties to avail yourselves once more of our cordial if humble hospitality," he said. "We are honored."

"Your Majesty's warriors have persuasive ways," replied Grandon. "Perhaps, now that you are Rogo, we can persuade you to permit us to depart to our own torrogat, where duty calls us."

"Perhaps," replied Thid Yet, dipping his thumb into a spore pod which one of the former slave girls of Yin Yin presented, and thrusting the red spores into his fat cheek. "Just what is your proposition?"

"Say, a million keds of gold."

"Humph! We are offered more for Her Majesty alone."

"Two million."

"Not enough."

"Three—"

"Wait," interrupted Thid Yet. "You but waste your breath. Her Majesty will remain here as was previously arranged, until it is time to take her to the rendezvous. Though she has been deprived of the pleasure of Yin Yin's company, we trust that we will make a satisfactory substitute."

"Why you—!" Grandon would have sprung at the throat of the man on the throne had he not been seized by the guards.

"One moment, Majesty. Permit me to finish. We are grieved that we can not entirely comply with your request, yet we will in part fulfill it."

"In part?"

"Yes. We will permit you to leave, but not for your own country. Although you left no witnesses, we have considerable evidence that it was you who beheaded our just and generous predecessor. We also remember that it was due to you that we nearly lost our own head. So we will allow you to leave— will, in fact, speed you on your way, for it would be dangerous to have you near us. But instead of sending you to your own torrogat, we will dispatch you to the Kingdom of Thorth."

Thorth being the Kingdom of Heaven, he beckoned to one of the two brawny guards who stood behind the throne—their immense two-handed scarbos much in evidence. "Come, Ez Bin. Clip me the head from this fine fellow, and see that you cut it cleanly, as I would retain it for a souvenir."

Swinging the heavy scarbo to his shoulder, the headsman marched forward. Grandon was quickly forced to his knees by his two guards. Ez Bin took a position beside him, tested the keenness of his blade with his thumb, and carefully measured the distance and position of Grandon's neck, closing one eye and squinting the other. Then, with the swift assurance of an expert, he raised his blade.

Vernia, who had been watching the scene, too horrified even to utter a sound, covered her eyes with her hands. Then she suddenly went limp in the hands of her two guards.

CHAPTER **XVIII**

THE ALLIES ATTACK

IN THE FLAGSHIP OF ZINLO OF OLBA rode Kantar the Gunner and Narine, looking down at the city of Huitsen through several feet of the lowest cloud stratum. The ship was flying in this stratum that it might remain invisible to the Huitsenni in the streets below, yet be able to keep watch. The offensive which the allies had planned the day before was now scheduled to take place.

Ten thousand of Reabon's brave warriors, guided by the Chispoks that San Thoy had selected, were converging on the city in an immense semicircle, and five thousand more, a contingent of Reabonian artillery, had their mattorks ready to make breaches in the walls and lay a barrage in front of the infantry as soon as the charge should commence or the enemy discover their presence.

Zinlo, who had been looking over the scene with his glass, said: "I wonder what has become of San Thoy and the two pirate vessels he was so positive he could bring through the gate. I see no sign of them in the canal. And our fleets still ride at anchor outside, waiting for our signal."

"Perhaps we should fly down and investigate," suggested Narine.

"Hardly," replied Kantar. "They would be sure to see us and precipitate a battle before we are ready."

"There's nothing to do but wait," said Zinlo, impatiently.

Meanwhile, San Thoy, standing in the commander's cabin of the foremost of the two ships which had been converted to the purpose of the allies, its crew augmented by a band of Reabonian warriors who kept out of sight below decks, and which was just then entering the fiord which led to Huitsen, was issuing swift orders to the mojak of the vessel. "Put three men on each oar," he commanded. "The steel bar which we are to drop between the stone gates to prevent their closing after us, is dragging on the bottom."

"Can we not raise it a trifle?" asked the mojak.

"No idiot. The guardians are already watching us. To touch those chains now would make them suspicious. Do as I say, and quickly, for the time for the offensive is almost at hand."

Under the added propulsion of the extra rowers, the boat moved slowly forward, dragging the heavy steel bar which the smiths of the fleet of Reabon had forged especially for this occasion by working all the previous night. Behind it came the second pirate ship, manned like the first by Chispoks culled from the two crews and a concealed contingent of Reabonian warriors. Its mojak, puzzled by the slow progress of the ship ahead, ordered his rowers to back water and wait until a suitable distance should be established between the two ships.

As San Thoy's vessel approached the massive stone gates, they did not open. Instead, there came a hail from one of the guardians.

"What ails you? Why do you move so slowly?"

"We were crippled in a battle with the Reabonian fleet," replied San Thoy. "Our hold is filling with water. Let us through quickly or we will sink and block the channel."

There was some delay. Evidently the guardians were not entirely satisfied with San Thoy's explanation. The mojak knew that they were being subjected to minute scrutiny from above.

"Fools!" he cried, at length. "Open the gate or the channel will be closed to all our ships. We are sinking rapidly. Besides, the enemy follows closely. Would you have them find us here?"

Evidently his words, or the fact that their rigging and upper works were damaged by shell-fire, decided the guardians, for the gates slowly slid apart.

San Thoy snapped an order to the rowers. "Pull, men, with all your might."

The channel was quite shallow here, and the bar dragged heavily, but the men worked with a will. Soon the boat was half through the gateway. "Now," commanded San Thoy, "let go the bar."

The chains were released, and struck the water with a loud splash.

"Ho, sailors. What was that you dropped?" one of the guards shouted from above.

Freed from the heavy drag of the bar, the ship shot forward under the exertion of the rowers. At the same time, its mattorks were trained on the grotto above, where the guards manipulated the machinery that worked the gates and kept watch for ships. Without replying to the question of the guard, the Chispoks opened fire.

The guards were sheltered behind a wall of stone, and in addition, were armed with mattorks. These instantly went into action, replying to the guns of San Thoy's ship and riddling her upper works with shells.

The second ship had, meanwhile, come up more slowly. Warriors clung to her masts and rigging. As she came halfway through the gate, she dropped anchor. The men in the rigging flung grappling-hooks up over the walls, and swarmed up the ropes. Many were hurled back, but enough succeeded in getting over to quickly conquer the guards. Then a mojo with twenty men took charge of the gate, and the two ships passed on through the immense black cavern.

Swiftly San Thoy ran to the foredeck of his craft. With an immense brush and a can of red pigment, he painted the word "open" in patoa, so it could be seen from the air. A moment later his craft nosed out into the canal. He dropped anchor about five hundred feet from the mouth of the cave and waited. Presently the other ship came up and anchored beside him.

A mojak with a company of warriors, whose duty it was to patrol the canal bank, came hurrying up and hailed him. "What was that firing?" he asked.

"We were pursued by the Reabonians," San Thoy replied. "They nearly had us. We just got through the gates in time."

"But did they not see the gates? Perhaps the secret way is not known to them."

"Perhaps," agreed San Thoy.

"You have lied to me," accused the mojak. "That firing was inside the cave."

"Go and see for yourself," suggested San Thoy.

"I will. Let me take a boat."

"Not you. You are too uncivil."

"Then I'll take one by force."

"Try it." San Thoy waved his hand, and fully two-score mattorks were trained on the mojak and his warriors. At this, the officer turned and whispered to a fat mojo who stood beside him. The fellow evidently counseled retreat, for they turned and marched away, leaving only a dozen men to watch the ships.

"They go to warn the city," said San Thoy's mojo.

"What odds?" replied San Thoy. "The mojak will order an investigation. A body of troops will be mobilized and marched back here. By that time our allies will have arrived, and the Reabonian army will be storming the city. Zinlo must have seen our signal, long since, and notified the fleets of Reabon, Tyrhana, and Adonijar."

Zinlo, in his aerial battleship, had ordered his commander to soar to the southeast of the city of Huitsen. They were hovering just above the ship canal. Kantar and Narine were watching the landscape below through one of the keel windows.

"Look!" cried Narine. "A ship is coming out of the cave."

Zinlo, who had been consulting with Lotar, seized his glasses and leveled them on the ship.

"It's San Thoy," he announced, "and the way is open. To the flagship of Ad, Lotar."

The ship shot forward with a tremendous burst of speed. In less than a minute it was far out over the Azpok, where the ships of the allies waited. The foremost of these was the flagship of Ad of Tyrhana.

With a swiftness that made Kantar's ears ring, the airship dropped. It came to a stop beside Ad's flagship as lightly as if it had fallen into a bed of thistledown.

Zinlo opened a side door. Not twenty feet from him, Ad stood on the foredeck of his fighting-craft.

"The way is open," announced the Prince of Olba.

"Good! I'll see you in the palace of Huitsen," replied Ad. Then he waved his hand to a sailor, who instantly ran a pennant to the masthead. Almost immediately, similar flags were hoisted by the other ships, showing that they had caught the signal. Then the sails were unfurled, and with the assistance of a swift landward breeze, the allied flotillas rapidly made their way toward the secret entrance to Huitsen.

Once more the flagship of Zinlo darted back above the city, this time just over the lowest cloud stratum. Here the air fleet of Olba hovered, waiting orders. The Torrogo's signal man stood forth on the deck just in front of the forward turret. In his right hand he held an immense red disk, and in his left, a yellow. He began making motions with one, then the other, then both, repeating them in numerous combinations which were evidently understood by the mojaks of the other battleships, as they immediately moved from their places and formed an immense circle which corresponded to the circumference of the city beneath. There they hovered, awaiting further orders.

Zinlo's own ship dropped once more into the lowest cloud stratum, high enough to be out of sight, but low enough so that he could watch developments. Presently another ship dropped down beside him. He opened a side door, and the commander of the ship did likewise.

"What news?" asked Zinlo.

"We caught up with the column of Ibbits, Your Majesty," replied the mojak. "Their Majesties of Reabon were not with them. The officer in command swore that Grandon of Terra had slain their Rogo and ridden away with his wife. He said they would have followed, but a blizzard obliterated the trail, so they decided to continue southward, bearing the body of their Rogo."

"Then what did you do?"

"We circled the snowy plain in all directions, and presently found a trail. From the tracks and kerra juice which spattered the snow, we knew it was the trail of a party of Huitsenni, mounted on zandars. It led us to the mouth of a cave, before which an enormous white strid lay dead. Inside the cave we found the smoldering remains of a web, the charred carcasses of three young strids, and a number of charred eggs.

"On coming out, however, we noticed and followed another trail, which led from a near-by cave. It was the trail of a man and woman. They had not returned to the cave from which they had come, neither were their remains in the cave of the strid; so we judged they had been captured by the party of mounted Huitsenni. The fact that the return trail of the yellow men led straight back to the city confirmed our belief."

"You have done well," said Zinlo. "Now take your squadron and get into the formation above. I'll signal you when to descend." He closed the door.

"Kantar, who had been listening to the conversation, said: "Your Majesty, I have a favor to ask."

"Name it," replied Zinlo. "You will deserve any favor within my power to confer."

"I would be set on one of the balconies of the palace of Huitsen, with two men to assist me."

"Impossible," replied Zinlo. "Our plans would be betrayed, and we would lose every advantage which a surprize attack would bring us."

"I am convinced, Majesty," said Kantar, "that Their Majesties of Reabon are prisoners in the palace. Grandon of Terra slew Yin Yin, Rogo of Huitsen. Under the circumstances, Yin Yin's successor can do no less than order his execution. Perhaps he has already done so, in which event I shall be too late. But I would be there to prevent it, if I can."

"What could three men do?"

"If I could reach one of the inner balconies that overlook the throne room with a man or two to guard my back and a tork in my hands, I could do much."

"You are right, Gunner. A tork in your hands is worth a hundred in the hands of ordinary men. And, after all, we're more anxious to save Grandon and Vernia than to take the city." He called to Lotar. "Send me two warriors. Then you will drop suddenly beside one of the outer balconies of the palace. As soon as the warriors have disembarked, you will swiftly return to this position."

"I hear and obey," replied Lotar.

Zinlo's orders were swiftly carried out.

Kantar bent over Narine's hand, but she snatched it free, and threw her arms around his neck.

"It may be that you go to your death, my brave gunner," she cried. "Hold me tight. Tell me again that you love me."

Zinlo halted the two warriors in the doorway. Then he coughed discreetly.

"We have arrived at the palace, Gunner. Come quickly, or we shall be shot down."

A side door was flung open. Her eyes sparkling with love and pride, Narine watched Kantar and the two warriors leap to the balcony. Then the door was closed, and before a single enemy mattork could be trained on it, the ship shot aloft and disappeared into the clouds.

Hovering there in the lower cloud stratum, Zinlo kept his glasses focused on the canal. Presently he cried: "There is Ad's flagship. Another follows, and another. It is time for the offensive."

He turned and gave swift orders to Lotar. The flagship rose above the first cloud stratum where the fleet waited, still in circular formation. The signal man flashed his red and yellow disks. Then Zinlo's ship took a place in the circle and began spiraling downward. Behind it followed the entire air fleet.

As soon as the flagship was through the lower cloud stratum, its keel mattorks went into action. The mattorks of the fleet instantly followed suit. There was a burst of flame from the ground beneath them as the Reabonian artillery opened fire, and great breaches began appearing in the city walls.

Then a long shout went up, and the long line of Reabonian infantry, which had been waiting in hiding, sprang forward, the light glinting from the barrels of its torks, and from its scarbos and long-bladed spears.

The ship canal was now filled with enemy vessels, following one another in close formation. Entering the landlocked harbor were the two captured pirate vessels—the first commanded by San Thoy.

The vessels which were anchored in the harbor immediately opened fire, concentrating on these two ships. San Thoy's vessel was riddled by shell-fire, and began to sink rapidly. He instantly ran it up beside an anchored vessel, and leading his mixed crew of white and yellow warriors, boarded the new craft. Only a few sailors were aboard, and these were quickly cut down.

In the meantime, the mighty flagship of Ad of Tyrhana had nosed into the harbor. The withering blasts from its heavy mattorks literally blew some of the smaller pirate craft out of the water, and wrought havoc with the larger vessels.

It was closely followed by the huge flagships of Reabon and Adonijar, whose powerful mattorks were equally efficient. And close on the heels of these, crowded the battleships of the allied fleet.

One by one, every pirate vessel that offered resistance was sunk or captured. Soon the allies were in complete command of the harbor. This accomplished, they landed warriors under cover of a heavy barrage, took the docks and warehouses with virtually no resistance, and marched into the city.

In the meantime, the Reabonian infantry was meeting with desperate resistance around the city walls. Time and again, Grandon's brave warriors charged into the breaches made by their artillery, only to be hurled back by the desperate defenders.

Presently, however, a contingent of fighting Traveks, Grandon's fierce warriors from the mountain fastnesses of Uxpo, broke through and charged straight for the palace.

The commander of the Huitsenni had anticipated just such an emergency, and was prepared to meet it. Mounted on zandars, firing their torks and brandishing their heavy scarbos, a yelling horde of reserves thundered straight at the charging Traveks.

The Uxponian mountaineers in the first line instantly knelt and presented their long-bladed spears, while their comrades immediately behind them fired over their heads at the swiftly approaching enemy. The two forces met with a terrific shock in which tough spear-shafts were splintered, scarbos flashed, and torks spat incessantly. In an instant the first line was a bloody shambles of dead and wounded men and zandars. At this point, wave after wave met, until the pile of dead, inextricably mingled with wounded men and maimed and struggling beasts, was so high that neither side could advance, both using it as a rampart over which to fire their torks.

The Reabonians, however, fighting shoulder to shoulder with their Uxponian brothers on either side, had quickly widened the breach made by the Traveks. Now they too, charged into the city, soon enveloping the mounted Huitsenni until all chance of retreat for the yellow cavalry was lost. Seeing that further resistance was hopeless, they threw down their arms, and clasped their hands behind their heads in token of surrender.

Leaving a few of their comrades to guard the prisoners and aid the wounded, the Traveks again charged forward with the Reabonians, helping to drive the yellow infantry toward the palace. "For Grandon and Vernia!" they shouted. "Down with Huitsen!"

From beyond the palace, a tremendous cheer answered them, as the allied warriors from the battleships drove the Huitsenni back.

While his keel mattorks kept up a continuous bombardment of the yellow army beneath, Zinlo watched these beginnings

of victory with satisfaction. Then he suddenly saw that for
which he had been waiting. Out from those buildings surrounding and closest to the palace, and from the fishing holes
in the vicinity, there appeared a swarm of Huitsenni, armed
and dressed like the others, with the exception that each man
wore a white scarf knotted around his neck and thrown over
his shoulders.

Part of this new force charged straight for the palace, and
the remainder formed a great skirmish line to cut off the approach of the retreating Huitsenni.

"It's the Chispoks!" cried Zinlo. "To the palace, Lotar."

C H A P T E R XIX

THE DUEL

BACK IN THE THRONE ROOM OF THID YET, Rogo of Huitsen, Grandon, who had been forced to his knees by his two burly guards, awaited the stroke of Ez Bin, the headsman. He saw the huge blade flash upward, and nerved himself for a mighty effort. As the two-handed scarbo descended, he flung himself backward, carrying both guards with him. The heavy blade crashed to the polished glass door, and many tiny cracks radiated from the point where it had struck.

Grandon instantly flung his right arm forward once more. The guard who clung to it tripped over the blade of Ez Bin, and losing his hold, fell on his face before the throne. His right arm now free, Grandon snatched the scarbo which depended from the belt of the other guard, and ran him through.

At this, one of Vernia's guards sprang forward and struck at Grandon with his scarbo. The Earth-man side-stepped the blow and countered with a slash to the head that stretched his opponent on the floor. In the meantime, Ez Bin had recovered his weapon, and made a terrific swing at Grandon's neck. Dodging beneath the blade, the Earth-man stabbed upward and thrust him through the throat. Then, before anyone could stop him, he sprang straight for the monarch who squatted on the throne.

With screams of terror, the slave girls scattered. But Thid Yet whipped out his scarbo and leaped to his feet. He had not been Rogo long enough to become fat and flabby like Yin Yin from easy living, nor was he a coward, but despite his great girth, a trained fighting man in the pink of condition, and the veteran of many hand-to-hand encounters which had made him the most feared duelist in Huitsen.

"Stand back," he shouted to the nobles and soldiers who had begun to crowd around. "Stand back and watch your Rogo carve the heart from this white-skinned slave who dares to attack the throne of Huitsen."

To the courtiers of Huitsen their ruler's word was absolutely law; so they fell back and made room for the two combatants. Nor were any of them worried as to the outcome. Thid Yet had not time to select any favorites from among those who stood about his throne, which he had seized with the assistance of the navy faction, nor had he, as yet, conferred any honors or promotions. If he were slain, another would take his place, probably no better or no worse, and Grandon could easily be dealt with.

It was evident, as Thid Yet sprang forward to meet the Earth-man, that despite Grandon's reputation as a swordsman, he was positive he could easily best him—that it would be an opportunity to add to his laurels and convince the Huitsenni beyond all doubt that they were ruled by a brave man.

As their blades clashed, and Grandon felt the strength of his wrist and met the lightning speed of his attack, he knew he had an opponent worthy of his steel, and that the outcome was indeed doubtful. Blood was drawn on both sides at the very start. First Thid Yet's point raked Grandon's cheek cutting a deep gash. Then the Earth-man countered with a swift head cut. The Rogo parried in time to save his head, but not his ear, which was shorn off by the blow.

The spectators cried out in delighted amazement at the swift and brilliant sword-play that followed. Trained from infancy in the use of the scarbo, these men of Huitsen knew that they were witnessing a duel the like of which they might never see again were they to live a dozen lifetimes. One after another, Grandon tried all the tricks he had learn from his old fencing master, Le Blanc, and from the numerous scarbo experts he had encounted. But thrust or cut as he would, the darting blade of Thid Yet was there to meet his, and to counter with a lightning slash or a swift riposte. Time and again Grandon received wounds which might have been fatal had he not succeeded in parrying them or springing back just in time. And for every wound he received, the yellow Rogo was dealt two, though he was equally successful in avoiding a fatal injury.

Bathed in blood and perspiration, the two contestants fought back and forth over an area that had become slippery with their own gore. Grandon's sword arm began to ache. His head swam dizzily. Loss of blood was beginning to sap his strength. He wondered how Thid Yet, who appeared to be losing more blood than he, could stand the terrific exertion. And wondering, he began to conserve his strength, to fight a defensive rather than an offensive battle, and to wait.

Presently the Earth-man felt the arm of his adversary begin to weaken. Still he fought cautiously, reserving his strength for a final effort—waiting. Suddenly Thid Yet extended his weapon in a vicious but clumsy thrust at Grandon's left breast.

With a quick parry, and a narrow moulinet ending in a swift, drawing cut, the Earth-man brought his keen blade down on his opponent's extended wrist, shearing through muscle and bone. The scarbo of the Rogo clattered to the floor, his severed hand still clinging to the grip.

Thid Yet uttered a grunt of surprise and pain, and stared at his spurting wrist for a moment as if he could not believe what he saw. Then he clamped the fingers of his left hand just behind the stump to stay the bleeding, and staggered backward, collapsed against the base of his throne.

In the uproar that followed, Grandon leaped back to where Vernia, who had recovered consciousness shortly after the duel commenced and watched it with bated breath, stood in the custody of her remaining guard. The fellow reached for his scarbo, but not quickly enough. He died with the blade half out of the scabbard and Grandon's point through his heart. With his left arm around his wife's slender waist, Grandon waved his bloody scarbo, menacing the nobles and warriors who were crowding around him.

One elevated his tork, but before he could use it, there was a report from an upper balcony, and he pitched forward on his face. A voice rang out from above them. "Back, all of you, and lay down your arms. The first to menace Their Majesties dies."

Looking up, Grandon saw Kantar standing on a balcony, his tork muzzle pointed over the railing. Behind him, two Olban warriors guarded the door.

A number of the nobles had rushed to Thid Yet's assistance. Two of them helped him to the throne, while a third tightly bound his wrist with a strip of silk torn from his own cloak. The cat-like eyes of the Rogo glittered with hatred.

"Shoot them," he groaned. "Slay them all."

A noble reached for his tork, followed by two more. But as swiftly as they went for their weapons, the tork of the gunner spoke. One after another they sank to the floor. The lesson

was not lost on the others. Most of them quickly complied
with Kantar's request by opening their belts and letting their
weapons drop to the floor. Then they clasped their hands behind their heads in token of surrender. A few guards who
had rushed in from the outer corridors to learn the cause of
the disturbance, quickly followed their example.

"What's this?" cried Thid Yet. "Is my entire court to be
captured by a single marksman?" He reached for his own
tork. Then a bullet drilled him neatly between the eyes and he
slumped forward, dead.

This settled the matter for those who had hesitated to obey
the commands of the sharp-shooting gunner. They all dropped
their weapons and clasped their hands behind their heads.

Leaving one of his companions to cover the group while
the other still watched the door, Kantar dropped from balcony
to balcony until he reached the floor. Scarcely had his feet
touched its mirrored surface when a terrific bombardment
commenced outside. He ran over to where Grandon and
Vernia stood, and made obeisance.

"What's all the shooting about outside?" asked Grandon.

"Your Majesty's warriors are attacking the city," replied
Kantar, "under cover of a barrage from the artillery. The air
fleet of Olba is also bombarding the city, as are the ships of
Reabon, Tyrhana, and Adonijar, which are now fighting their
way into the harbor and coming up the canal."

"But you! Where did you come from with these Olban
warriors? Did you drop from the sky?"

"In truth, I did, Majesty. Zinlo of Olba, at my request,
dropped me on one of the outer balconies of the palace with
these two warriors. His airship was not fired upon, as it came
and went so suddenly that the Huitsenni had no time to train
their heavy mattorks on it. I hoped to find you here, as a
squadron sent to follow the party of Ibbits with whom Your
Majesties were supposed to be traveling, returned to report that
you were not with them. I feared that your lives would be

put in jeopardy by the attack, and so came before the assault. By arguing with our scarbos, we convinced several yellow guards who barred our way that we had important business with the Rogo of Huitsen. Then we came to the inner balcony."

"You came in the nick of time, Gunner," said Grandon, "and I'm eternally grateful. Now, let's get out of here."

The gunner signaled to the Olban warrior on the balcony. He called to his companion, and the two dropped from balcony to balcony under the protection of the watchful gunner's tork, until they reached the floor.

"What shall we do with these prisoners, Majesty?" asked Kantar, indicating the group of disarmed nobles, officers, and slaves who still stood with their hands clasped behind their heads.

Grandon thought for a moment. "We'll take them with us," he decided. "It is the only way. Let the two Olban warriors bind their hands behind their backs."

While the members of the group were being bound with strips torn from their own clothing, Grandon selected a tork and ammunition belt from the pile of weapons. He also exchanged his nicked and bloody scarbo for a jewel-hilted weapon which had belonged to one of the nobles. Vernia also armed herself, and the two assisted Kantar to keep watch on the balconies and doorways. But it soon appeared that there was no need for this. Evidently the thunder of the conflict outside had prevented the palace inmates from taking any interest in what went on in the throne room.

As soon as the prisoners had been bound, Grandon divided them into two groups, one to march before them, and one behind. Then, with Grandon and Kantar covering the group that marched before and the two Olbans walking backward with their torks trained on those who came behind, they passed out into the corridor which led to the main gate.

They had scarcely moved twenty feet along this corridor, when a considerable body of Huitsenni, wearing white scarves around their necks, poured in from a side corridor. Grandon instantly elevated his tork, but Kantar, recognizing the white scarves as the symbol previously agreed upon, stayed his hand.

"Don't shoot, Majesty," he said. "These are friends." He called to the advancing warriors. "Ho, Chispoks. We are brothers and allies. Relieve us of these prisoners."

"Gladly, brothers. We were sent by Han Lay to rescue you, and assist in taking the palace, but you have evidently been able to take care of yourselves."

"Is the palace taken?" Grandon asked the mojak of the band.

The officer bowed low. "No, Majesty. But it soon will be. Already a thousand of the brotherhood have come in through the boat entrances, and they are fighting their way to the top. Five thousand more are storming the gates on the street level, and the rest stand ready to cut off the retreating army of Thid Yet."

"Then my soldiers have broken through?"

"They have, Majesty, and drive the army of the false Rogo before them like frightened frellas, while the warriors from the ships close in from the other side."

"The false Rogo is now a dead Rogo," Grandon told him. "But where is Han Lay?"

"He was to lead the charge on the palace gate, so it is there he will be if he has not fallen."

"Then let us charge through from the inside. It will make victory swifter and easier."

"But most of my men are fighting on the upper floors."

"Never mind. Can you spare twenty?"

"Assuredly. Fifty."

"Splendid! I will lead them." He turned to the two Olbans, who, relieved of their prisoners, awaited orders. "Guard Her Majesty well," he commanded. Then to Kantar. "Come, Gunner."

Followed by the fifty men whom the mojak had detailed to accompany them, Grandon and Kantar led the charge through the entrance, and straight into the mêlée where the palace guards strove with the Chispoks at the gate. For some minutes the guards, beset from both sides, offered half-hearted resistance. Then, one by one, they threw down their weapons and clasped their hands behind their heads. The attacking Chispoks surged in, with Han Lay at their head.

"I rejoice to find you alive, Majesty," said Han Lay, rendering the royal salute to Grandon.

"And I, you, Your Majesty soon to be," replied Grandon, returning his salute.

Suddenly a string of aerial battleships dropped down from the sky and circled the palace. Swiftly their mattorks silenced the weapons of those who fired at them. Then they sailed up to the balconies at the various levels, and Olban warriors poured down their aluminum stairways into the palace. The leading airship settled beside the palace gate. The steps dropped, and down them came Zinlo and Narine.

Grandon and Zinlo saluted each other in the Zorovian fashion, then puzzled those who stood around them by enthusiastically shaking hands, a purely earthly demonstration which was unknown on Venus.

"I see that you are in at the kill, in spite of the fact that we couldn't notify you," said Zinlo.

"Decidedly," replied Grandon. "Where are Ad and Aardvan?"

"Coming. They have just accepted the surrender of the Romojak of Huitsen, and will be here in a moment."

Grandon presented Han Lay to Zinlo and Narine. Then Vernia came out, accompanied by her two Olban guards, and to her he was also presented.

A moment later, three men strode up to the palace gate, a half-dozen warriors making way for them through the vast multitude that had gathered there. They were Ad of Tyrhana,

Aardvan of Adonijar, and San Thoy. Grandon held a short conference with his allies. Then, accompanied by Han Lay, he mounted to the top step of the aluminum stairs which led to Zinlo's flagship. It was a position from which he could command a view of the entire crowd, and be seen by them.

"People of Huitsen," he shouted. "First of all, I want to tell you, and I speak on behalf of my allies as well as myself, that we are not here to exact tributes or reparations, nor to gloat over a prostrate foe. On the contrary, we wish to establish friendly relations with the people of Huitsen—relations that will last through the years. The officer and renowned warrior who stands here beside me is willing to meet the conditions which will best foster these relations, namely, an abolition of piracy, the freeing of all slaves who have been acquired by buccaneering and coastal raids, and the entry of Huitsen into peaceful commerce with the other nations of this planet.

"Being in full accord with these policies, we will withdraw our warriors as soon as a treaty is concluded with him, if you will acclaim him your Rogo. What is your pleasure?"

"Han Lay for Rogo," shouted a warrior, and the shout was taken up by a thousand throats.

Presently Grandon held up his hand for silence. When the clamor had ceased, he said: "Have you any other candidates to propose?"

No one spoke. He waited for a moment. "Then acclaim him," he cried.

"Hail Han Lay, Rogo of Huitsen!" roared the crowd, as with one voice.

When the shouting had subsided to a murmur, Grandon turned to Han Lay, and said: "I have a suggestion, Your Majesty. There is one who, though he has his little weaknesses, has been largely instrumental in the consummation of this glorious victory. I refer to San Thoy, and recommend that he be suitably rewarded."

The new Rogo beckoned to San Thoy, who came and made obeisance before him.

"Rise, San Thoy, Romojak of the Navies of Huitsen," said Han Lay.

Then he and Grandon descended the ladder, and amid the cheering of the populace, the royal group, attended by their officers and guards, went into the palace.

As they entered, Han Lay, who was walking beside Grandon, said: "What of this lascivious Rogo who was the cause of Her Majesty's abduction? Can we be of assistance in bringing him to justice?"

"You can, decidedly," replied Grandon. "I had already thought of a plan. I should like to borrow one of your largest vessels complete with officers and crew, with San Thoy in command. Also, if you can furnish me with a sculptor who can make a life-like image of one who will pose for him, say in wax, or some such material, I shall be able to complete my plans without great difficulty."

"These are but trifles," protested Han Lay. "A ship will be put at your disposal immediately, and within the hour a dozen such sculptors as you require will await your pleasure."

"Excellent! As soon as I have had these scratches dressed, I'll explain my plan to you."

CHAPTER XX

RETRIBUTION AND REWARD

TEN DAYS HAD ELAPSED SINCE THE FALL of Huitsen. On the day following their victory, the ships and warriors of the allies had sailed away. Only a part of the Olban air fleet remained, while Grandon, Vernia, Zinlo, Loralie, Kantar, and Narine stayed at the palace as the guests of the new Rogo. Now Han Lay stood on the palace steps, surrounded by his nobles and officers, to bid his friends farewell.

Zinlo's flagship had descended to the ground, and two of its aluminum staircases had been lowered. Up one of these a number of Huitsenni struggled with two heavy, coffin-like chests, and passed them to the waiting Olbans.

Farewells were said, and, one by one, Han Lay's guests mounted the other stairway. The stairs were raised, the doors were closed, and the mighty airship shot skyward, while the people cheered and the palace mattorks thundered a farewell salute.

At an elevation of about two thousand feet, the flagship darted seaward, followed by the fleet, which had been hovering above the palace.

Installed in his luxurious cabin, Zinlo's guests sipped kova and chatted gayly. Having seen to their comforts, the Torrogo of Olba climbed to the forward turret to note their progress.

Presently Grandon joined him. "Are you sure we can catch San Thoy before he reaches the rendezvous," he asked.

"Positive," Zinlo replied. "We have already covered half the distance."

"Marvellous! How fast will these things go, anyway?"

"Earth distance and time, about a thousand miles an hour. In Olba, the speed is reckoned in rotations of the planet at its equator, or fractions thereof. Our smallest and slowest ships make at least a quarter of a rotation. This one can easily do a rotation."

"I thought the shoreline of Huitsen receded pretty fast, but I didn't know it was quite that speedy. Look! We're passing over a fleet, now."

"That's Ad of Tyrhana, ready to attack Zanaloth from the south. See that fleet over to the west? That's Aardvan spoiling for a fight. Your own ships are over at your right, and the fleet that set sail from Reabon under your orders should be within twenty-five miles of the north coast of the Island of the Valkars by now."

"Why, there's San Thoy's ship, already."

"Right. We'll ascend and do a little scouting before we drop you off."

He gave several swift orders to his Romojak. Then the entire fleet of aircraft shot skyward, and entered the lowest cloud stratum.

Looking down through the thin veil of vapor, Grandon presently descried an island, the Island of the Valkars. Anchored off its tiny harbor was a single battleship, flying the flag of Mernerum. But behind a jutting promontory, only a little way off, fully fifty big battleships lurked.

"It's just as you thought," said Zinlo, at sight of the concealed ships. "Either Zanaloth was afraid of treachery on the part of the Huitsenni, or he intended treachery toward them. He came prepared for trouble, in any event."

They cruised toward the north a few minutes longer, and Grandon saw another fleet, consisting of fully a hundred splendid battleships, the pride of Reabon's navy, sailing toward the island. Zinlo saw them, too, and immediately gave orders to turn back.

"All is ready," he said. "Now, if you still insist, I'll put you on San Thoy's ship, but I can't for the life of me see the sense of it. We've got them bottled up, anyway, and it won't be much of a job to lick them."

"I'll tell you why I insist on carrying out my plan," replied Grandon. "It's the only way I can make sure of meeting my worst enemy face to face."

"I see. You want the pleasure of killing him, yourself. Well, I don't blame you."

They paused, at this moment, above the bat-winged vessel which Han Lay had lent to Grandon, and Zinlo gave orders for them to descend.

Lightly the airship dropped beside the vessel. Grappling-irons were tossed aboard, and the two stairways let down. Grandon bade his friends good-bye, and took Vernia in his arms. She clung to him at the door—begged him not to go.

"You are putting your head in the mouth of a marmelot," she said. "Why not capture him first, then deal with him afterward? I'm afraid for you."

"And I," replied Grandon, "am afraid he might otherwise escape me. This way, he will not."

As he descended the ladder, San Thoy stood on the deck to greet him, mumbling kerra spores and grinning toothlessly. In the meantime, the two casket-like chests which had been brought in the airship were lowered to the deck of the vessel. The stairs were drawn up and the grappling irons cast off.

Grandon waved farewell to his friends, and entered the cabin of the bowing San Thoy.

Zanaloth, dissolute Torrogo of Mernerum, sat at the gold-topped table in the luxurious cabin of his flagship, sipping kova. Oglo, Romojak of the Imperial Navy, stood at attention, awaiting his pleasure.

Presently the dissipated Torrogo turned his bloated counten-ance toward his chief naval officer, and said: "The time is nearly at hand, Oglo. Are you positive that everything is ready?"

"Positive, Your Majesty. A thousand warriors are concealed in the hold, awaiting instructions. Our fleet lurks in readiness to come to us under full sail at the boom of the first mattork."

Zanaloth emptied his kova bowl and smacked his thick, senu-ous lips. "Very good. Very good, indeed. If the pirates come in a single ship, as we agreed, we can capture it. If they mean treachery, and have other vessels standing by to attack us, they will be easily taken care of by our battle fleet.

"Now let us review your instructions, so there will be no mistakes. As soon as the pirates display the royal prisoner, we will request that she be brought aboard our vessel. They, on their side, will no doubt insist that the gold be transferred to their ship. We will agree to this, and begin transferring the gold. But as soon as the Princess of Reabon is safely inside this cabin, I will enter in and close the door. That will be your signal to attack. Let the warriors take the place of the gold-passers, and charge into the other ship. See that you have plenty of grappling irons aboard her, so she cannot slip away from us. And don't forget to go into action immediately with the mattorks, so the battle fleet will know they are to start at once."

"To hear Your Majesty is to obey," replied Oglo.

"And remember. Every man aboard the pirate vessel must die. If need be, we will sink their ship, but first we must try to get back what gold has been taken aboard her. As for the slaves we are supposed to have put ashore for them, the pirates will not live to look for them. We will have both the girl and the gold, and the Rogo of Huitsen will perhaps guess that he has been beaten at his own game, but he will have no proof."

"I will not forget, Majesty."

"If your head fails you in this, I promise it will no longer remain on your shoulders to trouble you. Go, now, and watch for that ship."

Oglo made profound obeisance, and withdrew.

Zanaloth fidgeted impatiently. Presently he quaffed another bowl of kova and getting ponderously to his feet, paced the floor.

Suddenly the door was flung open, and Oglo, bowing on the threshold announced breathlessly: "A sail, Majesty! A pirate sail!"

Zanaloth grunted. "So! They come to the rendezvous at last."

He squeezed his ample girth through the doorway, and walked forward, Oglo following at a respectful distance. Then he took the glass which his romojak obsequiously proffered, and focused it on the approaching vessel. Traveling under full sail before a stiff breeze, it was making considerable speed.

"Bones of Thorth!" he exclaimed. "We must save that splendid ship, if possible. It flies over the water like an ormf. A few alterations, and it will never be recognized."

As if its commander had no suspicion of treachery, the pirate ship sailed swiftly up to them, hove to, and dropped its anchors. An officer came out of a cabin, wearing the uniform of a romojak, and Zanaloth hailed him.

"Are you Thid Yet, Romojak of Huitsen," he asked.

"No, I am San Thoy, Romojak of Huitsen," was the reply. "Thid Yet is dead, and I have come to keep the rendezvous in his place."

"You have brought the royal slave-girl?"

"We have, Your Majesty. And what of the gold?"

"We stand ready to deliver it to you. But first let me see the royal prisoner."

"What of the slaves you were to place on the island for us?"

"They are there, under guard, awaiting your pleasure. But let us see your prisoner."

"Very well, Majesty."

San Thoy went into a cabin, and remained for several minutes. Then he came out, alone. "She has fainted, Your Majesty. Will you not come aboard and see her?"

"Ha! What's this? Perhaps you have not brought her, after all."

"Well then, if you doubt my word, I'll have her carried out, so you may view her."

He raised his hand, and a mojak entered the cabin. He came out in a moment, followed by four Huitsenni, who bore a litter on which reposed the golden-haired, richly clad figure of a young woman.

Zanaloth stared until he was watery-eyed. Then he focused his glass on the recumbent figure and stared again.

"By the blood and body of Thorth!" he exclaimed to Oglo. "It is she. It must be. For nowhere on Zorovia is there beauty such as hers." To San Thoy he called: "I am satisfied. Let us draw the ships together with grappling irons. My men are ready to unload the gold."

Irons were quickly hurled from ship to ship, and the chains, drawn taut by hand-turned winches, gradually drew the two vessels together. This achieved, gang-planks were dropped across, fore and aft, and Zanaloth's men began carrying bars of gold to the pirate ship from the after hold, to be checked, weighed, and received by members of the yellow crew.

For some time Zanaloth and San Thoy chatted across the rails. Then the latter said: "Nearly half the gold is unloaded. Shall we convey Her Majesty to the quarters you have provided for her?"

This was precisely what Zanaloth wanted, but he did not wish to appear too eager. "At your convenience," he replied. "The cabin behind me has been prepared for her."

San Thoy signaled to the officer who stood near the recumbent figure. The officer gave a command, and four Huitsenni took up the litter, while four more came out from the cabin and fell in behind them with a heavy, ornate chest about seven feet in length.

"What is in that chest?" asked Zanaloth, suspiciously.

"A few of Her Majesty's belongings," replied San Thoy. "Mostly wearing apparel and ornaments."

San Thoy himself crossed the gang-plank ahead of the others.

"This cabin?" he asked, indicating the door of Zanaloth's cabin.

"That is right. Just leave her in there, and I'll call the ship's doctor to attend her in a moment."

Zanaloth drank in the beauty of the recumbent girlish form as it was borne past him. "How still she is!" he thought. "Perhaps she is dead, and they have tricked me." But a searching look at the red lips and pink cheeks reassured him. "No corpse could have such bloom of life and health as this," he reasoned.

Under the supervision of their officer, the eight men placed the litter and the large chest in the cabin. Then they retired.

"You will excuse me," said Zanaloth, formally, "if I go to examine the merchandise I have purchased at so high a price."

"Assuredly," replied San Thoy. "I will, in the meantime, take a closer look at the gold with which it was purchased."

He bowed low, with right hand extended palm downward, and turning, crossed the plank to his own ship.

Zanaloth watched his broad back with a supercilious sneer, until he had reached his own vessel. Then, with a significant glance at Oglo, he swung on his heel, and entering his cabin, slammed the door shut behind him. The boom of a mattork outside, instantly followed his action. It was succeeded by shouts, commands, shrieks, and groans, mingled with the popping of torks, the clash of blades, the scurrying feet on deck, and the rumble of mattorks. He smiled cunningly as he thought of the splendid prize which his concealed warriors would take so easily, and of the very slight expense at which he had been to secure the golden-haired beauty who lay at his mercy on the litter before him.

He crossed the room, and kneeling, touched a rosy cheek. Then he drew back his hand with a sharp exclamation of surprize. The face was as hard and cold as if it had been hewn from marble.

A heavy hand fell on his shoulder and closed with a grip that made him wince. He was jerked to his feet, and spun around to face a tall, handsome stranger, who wore the scarlet of royalty and the insignia of the imperial house of Reabon.

"Who—who are you?" he stammered, his trembling voice barely audible above the din of battle outside.

"I am Grandon of Terra, Torrogo of Reabon, and husband of her whom you would have wronged—whose graven image you just now profaned by the touch of your filthy hand."

Behind Grandon, the ornate chest under which the four Huitsenni had staggered stood with the lid thrown back, empty. Zanaloth's gaze roved from this to the door, as he realized the manner in which Grandon had gained access to his cabin. He leaped for the door, but found it locked. Grandon reached in his belt-pouch and held up the key.

"Wha—what do you want?" asked Zanaloth.

"I have come for your head," replied the Earth-man, whip-

"*He drew back his hand with a sharp exclamation of surprize. The face was as hard and cold as if it had been hewn from marble.*"

Chapter XX.

ping out his scarbo. "On guard, if you have the manhood left to defend it."

With trembling fingers, Zanaloth drew his own scarbo. In his youth he had been accounted an excellent scarboman. But that day was long past. Years of dissipation and luxurious living had made him short of breath and flabby of muscle. And he knew that there were few, if any, of the most expert duelists on Zorovia who could meet Grandon of Terra, scarbo in hand, and live to boast of it. Only a trick, a sudden, unexpected move, might save him. He came on guard, but before the blades had touched, lowered his point.

"You may choose between—" Grandon began. But just then Zanaloth raised his weapon and lunged at his opponent's unprotected body. Grandon had no time to parry this vicious and cowardly thrust. Barely in time to avert disaster, he hurled himself to one side, so that the point only grazed him. Zanaloth automatically recovered his stance as Grandon now attacked. For a moment, it seemed to the Mernerumite that the blade of his opponent had wrapped itself around his own. Then his weapon was twisted from his grasp, and flew through the air alight in a corner of the cabin. Zanaloth started back, his eyes wide with terror, as the point of the Earth-man plunged straight for his breast. But Grandon stopped the thrust, and contented himself with merely touching his antagonist.

The din of battle had increased outside, but neither man heeded it.

"I suggest that you pick up your scarbo," said Grandon, "and that hereafter you keep a tighter grip on it."

Furtively watching his generous opponent, Zanaloth slunk to the corner and recovered his weapon. He knew that he could not hope to win this fight, that death had him marked for its own. Great beads of sweat standing out on his forehead betrayed the fear that gripped his craven heart.

At his left side, as at Grandon's, there hung a jeweled, gold-plated tork. Suddenly he lowered his left hand, gripped the weapon, and was about to press the firing-button when a projectile struck his wrist, numbing it, and paralyzing his fingers. With incredible swiftness, Grandon had again forestalled him.

Seeing that he had rendered the Mernerumite's tork hand useless, Grandon lowered his own weapon. "Since you can no longer fight with the tork," he said, politely, "perhaps we had best resume with the scarbo." He advanced, and once more their blades met. "I advise you," continued Grandon, mechanically cutting, thrusting, and parrying, "to guard well your head, as I have promised it to the Rogo of Huitsen. A little gift to recompense him for the loss of much gold and many slaves. But then the head of a Torrogo is a rare and truly royal gift, even if its intrinsic worth is trifling."

Zanaloth said nothing. He was fighting with all his strength, yet the Earth-man was only playing with him. Suddenly Grandon's blade flashed in a swift moulinet, touched the Mernerumite's neck, and was withdrawn, without so much as drawing blood. But to Grandon's surprize, his antagonist dropped his weapon and sank to the floor, limp, and apparently lifeless.

For some time the Earth-man stood there, waiting, suspecting a trick. But as his opponent continued motionless, he bent and felt a flabby wrist, then held his hand over the heart. There was no pulse. Zanaloth of Mernerum was dead, not slain by the scarbo, but by a weapon that is often more deadly, that always tortures before it kills—fear.

Grandon rose to his feet and sheathed his bloodless blade. Then, taking the key from his belt pouch, he opened the cabin door and stepped out on deck. San Thoy was waiting there to greet him. The fighting had ceased, and the Huitsenni worked side by side with his own Fighting Traveks who had been concealed in the hold of their ship. They were tossing the corpses of the slain Mernerumites overboard, tending the wounded, and guarding the prisoners.

A large aerial battleship dropped beside them. Grappling-irons were cast aboard, and an aluminum stairway was lowered. Zinlo stood in the doorway.

"The battle fleet of Mernerum has surrendered," he said. "Coming aboard?"

"Immediately," replied Grandon. With one foot on the stairway, he turned to San Thoy. "Good-bye, my friend," he said. "Come and visit me in Reabon. Oh, by the way! You will find the gift I promised Han Lay on the floor of Zanaloth's cabin. Present it to him with my compliments."

San Thoy bowed low, and grinned toothlessly, as Grandon mounted the stairs.

The next day, Grandon sat at the crystal-topped table in the drawing-room of his private apartments in the imperial palace of Reabon.

Bonal, his torrango, or prime minister, appeared in the doorway and made obeisance. "The messenger has arrived from Mernerum, Your Majesty," he announced.

"I'll receive him here," replied Grandon. "And by the way, Zonal, ask Zinlo of Olba to come in now. I want him to be present at the interview."

A few moments later, Bonal announced: "His Imperial Majesty, Zinlo of Olba, and Mojak Sed of the staff of Orthad, Supreme Romojak of Reabon."

Zinlo entered, followed by a young Reabonian officer. The Torroga of Olba took a seat at the table, and the democratic Grandon invited the young officer also to be seated, knowing it would not offend his equally democratic guest.

"You bring a message from Orthad?" Grandon asked.

"I do, Majesty. He bids me inform you that we took Mernerum with ease. The people were sick of the tyrannous Zanaloth, and most of them actually welcomed us. We were delayed only by the difficulties which arise in moving so large an army. The fighting was but desultory, and there were few casualties."

"What was the attitude of the nobles and officials?"

"They begged that Mernerum be annexed to Reabon, or if this should not comport with Your Majesty's wishes, that you name a competent Torrogo to rule them. So as soon as Kantar the Gunner arrived in the Olban airship, His Excellency named him Torrogo, in accordance with Your Majesty's commands. He was later acclaimed by the nobles, warriors, and people without a dissenting voice."

"What of the other ceremony?"

"It has been performed, Majesty. And Her Majesty invites all to attend the feast which will be held this evening."

"Did you bring with you a messenger from the new Torroga?"

"I did, Your Majesty. He awaits your permission to present his missive to Ad of Tyrhana."

"Good. You may go now. And send this messenger to me."

The mojak arose, and making the customary obeisance, withdrew.

"Thus far," Grandon told Zinlo, "our plot has worked out. It remains to be seen how Ad of Tyrhana will take the news." He called a guard. "Have Bonal usher in Their Majesties of Tyrhana and Adonijar," he commanded.

"I can tell you how Ad will take it," said Zinlo. "He'll take it as a marmelot takes a slap on the nose. But it was the only thing to do."

A moment later, Ad and Aardvan were ushered in by Bonal. A slave brought kova, and the four Torrogos were chatting merrily over their bowls when Bonal announced: "A messenger from Her Imperial Majesty for the Torrogo of Tyrhana."

"What's this?" exclaimed Ad. "I didn't know Zanaloth left a widow. And why should she send a messenger to me?"

"Perhaps an interview with the messenger will explain," rumbled the deep voice of Aardvan.

"True. Show him in, Bonal."

The messenger, who wore the uniform of a mojak of the Imperial Guards of Mernerum, made obeisance to all four of the rulers. His puzzled look showed that he did not know which one to address.

"I am the Torrogo of Tyrhana," said Ad. "I believe your message is for me."

"It is, Your Majesty." The mojak took a small scroll from his belt pouch and handed it to Ad. "From Her Imperial Majesty, the Torroga of Mernerum," he said.

Ad broke the seal and unrolled the missive. First he looked puzzled, then astounded, then fiercely angry. His face purpled and his brow contracted. "Blood of Thorth!" he exploded. "Narine has eloped with that young upstart of a gunner, and married him!"

"She could have done worse," soothed Grandon. "The gunner is now Torrogo of Mernerum."

"The little she-marmelot! The traitor! The ungrateful child! I'll disown her! I'll—I'll—"

"Tut, tut," said Aardvan. "I think she has made a splendid match."

"But what of Gadrimel? What of our pact that my daughter and your son should wed?"

"I don't like to mention this," replied Aardvan, but Gadrimel picked up a slave-girl in Huitsen and brought her here with him. Zena, I believe he called her, an ex-concubine of Yin Yin's. I told him to get rid of her, and last night they both disappeared. Later, I learned that they had gone for a cruise in one of my ships."

"Um," grunted Ad, non-committally.

"So you see," continued Aardvan, "Their marriage would have been impossible, anyway. Besides, we need no marriage to comment the firm friendship between us. And think, you will now have as an additional ally the wealthy and powerful Torrogo of Mernerum, your son-in-law."

"That's right, Your Majesty," said Zinlo. "Forgive the child, and let's pile into one of my ships and attend the wedding feast tonight, all of us."

"What! You, too? This has all the earmarks of a conspiracy," said Ad.

Grandon filled the kova bowls all around, then took up his own, and said: "My friends, let us drink to the health and happiness of the charming young bride and the lucky bridegroom."

Zinlo and Aardvan drained their bowls.

Ad hesitated for a moment, then caught up his own bowl and emptied it with apparent gusto. "Our work is done," he said. "The power of the pirates is broken, and the port of peril is no more. Let us on to the wedding feast."